MORE WRONGS:
THE REVENGE

ANTHONY L. BAKER

Order this book online at www.trafford.com
or email orders@trafford.com

Most Trafford titles are also available at major online book retailers.

© Copyright 2017 Anthony L. Baker.

All rights reserved. No part of this publication may be reproduced, stored in a retrieval system, or transmitted, in any form or by any means, electronic, mechanical, photocopying, recording, or otherwise, without the written prior permission of the author.

Print information available on the last page.

ISBN: 978-1-4907-8528-8 (sc)
ISBN: 978-1-4907-8529-5 (hc)
ISBN: 978-1-4907-8540-0 (e)

Library of Congress Control Number: 2017916286

Because of the dynamic nature of the Internet, any web addresses or links contained in this book may have changed since publication and may no longer be valid. The views expressed in this work are solely those of the author and do not necessarily reflect the views of the publisher, and the publisher hereby disclaims any responsibility for them.

Any people depicted in stock imagery provided by Thinkstock are models, and such images are being used for illustrative purposes only.
Certain stock imagery © Thinkstock.

Trafford rev. 11/03/2017

Trafford PUBLISHING® www.trafford.com

North America & international
toll-free: 1 888 232 4444 (USA & Canada)
fax: 812 355 4082

CONTENTS

Chapter 1:   Pretty good. 1
Chapter 2:   Make you talk 5
Chapter 3:   Can't Stay Away 10
Chapter 4:   Nice & Fun 14
Chapter 5:   E. T. A. 17
Chapter 6:   New Order 20
Chapter 7:   Independence 24
Chapter 8:   Shot Caller 27
Chapter 9:   Are you crazy? 33
Chapter 10: Visitations 37
Chapter 11: I can perpetrate, too! 41
Chapter 12: SOLD! 44
Chapter 13: Bearing Gifts 48
Chapter 14: Two steps ahead 51
Chapter 15: Playa 54
Chapter 16: Can't I have both? 57
Chapter 17: On Record 60
Chapter 18: Major Roles 62
Chapter 19: Legalities 65
Chapter 20: Action Jackson 68
Chapter 21: Dirty Laundry 70
Chapter 22: 222 Reasons 73
Chapter 23: Sick call 76
Chapter 24: Wasted energy 79
Chapter 25: Boy Scout 82
Chapter 26: Plans change 86
Chapter 27: Restored order 91

Chapter 28: Finalization 95
Chapter 29: Up To Speed 98
Chapter 30: #StayWoke 102
Chapter 31: Act one 106
Chapter 32: The inquisition 109
Chapter 33: Family reunion 113
Chapter 34: In control 117
Chapter 35: Superior beings 122
Chapter 36: Karma.. 126
Chapter 37: No sensible answers 131
Chapter 38: R. I. P. 135
Chapter 39: Bee-otch!..139
Chapter 40: Hero 142
Chapter 41: All the fixings 145
Chapter 42: Gang bang..150
Chapter 43: Surprise!...155

About The Author..163

I would like to dedicate this book to my wife for her love and support.

CHAPTER 1

PRETTY GOOD.

Four years, nine months. Not a long time. Time enough, however, to get to know someone. Time enough to get to know a son. Time enough to get to know yourself. Your true self. Vincent Taylor; V for short, was feeling generous this morning, so he went to the kitchen of his newly built home and fixed breakfast. Since he and Terri had been travelling the world, V felt it was high time for them to settle down… especially since they had a child together. It didn't seem right to raise him without any stability or a true house for a home. V made sure that he didn't pattern his new home after his brother's ten thousand square foot home. That was just too big for V, so he built a four-bedroom, three-bathroom home with a treated wood deck on the back. The front would have a combination of redwood and gray brick. He allowed Terri to put her design thumbprint on the interior and also allowed for her to have the size of a kitchen she desired. He didn't put in a swimming pool, though. If they wanted to go swimming, they could just visit Jr. and Pat year-round, since their pool was inside and heated.

Terri and his son were still sleep, so this was the best time for V to make a move. Even though years had passed, this lifestyle was still new to him. He was rich beyond his wildest dreams… in more ways than just money. He was able to officially fix it where Terri was no longer married to his brother Victor, and now V and she could legally be together. Since they could be, he did the honorable thing…he married Terri. He was the new owner of a security system company; one he funded and started himself. He had a bouncing baby boy…well, he was already past the terrible two stages, so he wasn't bouncing anymore…unless one wanted to say that he was bouncing all over the place. V built himself his new home, ten miles from "his" previous home...well, his brother's previous home. He was close to his best friend, Jr., who now owned the previously mentioned house and now V could see Moms when he wanted, since she stayed in the same house as always. Anything would have been better than being in jail, but this? He hadn't anticipated this. This was Heaven on Earth! He loved his family and he could feel the love from them... especially Terri. Thanks to his brother's underhanded dealings, V was very wealthy, and even though the dealings were suspect, the outcomes became absolutely legal and V faced no harm or any repercussions for wrongdoings. Things were going pretty good for V right now. He couldn't help but think about his good fortunes constantly, but he was interrupted in his reflections by a kind, sleepy but familiar voice.

"Morning, baby." Terri entered the kitchen, rubbing her eyes, just as V was scrambling the eggs.

"Hey, Sugar! How'd you sleep?" V asked.

"Like a princess. Or a queen. Anyone with royalty status."

"Oh? And why would that be?"

"Because, I'm married to the Prince of my heart; the King of my castle; the man of my dreams!" she said.

"Oh, so I'm the shit, huh?!"

"Yes, you are so full of shit, V," Terri said playfully.

"That's not what I said, and you know it."

"Yeah, I know," she replied.

V just smiled. He had never been in a relationship like this one and even though he thought he loved Cassie, he had never loved like this before. He also didn't think he'd really be married...even if he was going to ask Cassie when he got out of prison. And to think, he was now married to his brother Victor's former wife! This might seem strange to some, but V had experienced much stranger things in his life. He placed a plate of a full-size breakfast in front of her.

"Say, Terri, can we talk?"

"Sure, Sugar. Anytime."

"We've sure had ourselves an adventure, haven't we? You know, the travel; the gifts; the lavish life, so to speak?"

"I've enjoyed myself. You're quite the gentleman, V. Who knew that about you?"

"Well, I knew it about myself, but that's beside the point. What I was saying, was that you realize we have a whole lot of money and I really don't have to work another day in my life, if I chose not to, right?"

"Yeah, I know that. But I also know that you're not lazy and a little bit smarter than people gave you credit for. You can't sit on your ass all year and when tax time comes, you got nothing to show the IRS as an income. That's smart to start your own business, V. If it builds, then when you spend money, it won't look suspicious and the IRS will have something tangible to try to take all your money from."

"Ha, ha, that's funny. You're right, baby. I can't live in a house like this, drive cars like I drive and wear the finest clothes without showing a source. COC is doing good, too!"

"I know. I've seen the books, remember?"

"Yeah, that's right. I might need you to fill in for me this coming week. Moms might need me to help her with a catering job. You down?"

"For you? Hell, yeah! As much as you've done for me and Vas…shit, I'd be crazy not to help you out sometimes."

"You're already crazy."

"Why do you say that?"

"Because you married me."

"Well, if that's the case, then I'm crazy in love with you."

V paused.

"Terri? So, you're glad you're with me, huh?"

"I am."

"You do realize that I am not the man you met in law school, right?" V asked.

"I know that. I just wish you would stop bringing it up. I'm with who I wanted to be with all the time…or who I needed to be with. At least I'm with who I thought I was getting with in the first place. That bastard!"

"Okay, okay. Sorry for making you think about him. I'll try not to do it anymore. But since we are on the subject, and before we put this behind us, can I ask you another question?"

Terri looked up from the plate that V placed in front of her.

"What? About Victor?"

"Well…yeah."

"Damn. I guess so."

"Do you ever miss him? I mean, just a little bit?" V asked, not really wanting to know the answer.

Terri took a bite of her bacon and then took a big swig of orange juice.

"Boy! Now that is some good orange juice!" Terri commented.

V just looked at her. He knew his twin hurt her. Victor hurt V, too. V made him pay, though…for both of them. He thought, *Hell, maybe seeing me **is** hard enough, knowing that my brother and I look just alike. I'm not realizing how hard this must be…even if it **has** been over four years.*

"Yeah, that's the shit right there!" That's all V could respond with. Why ruin a good moment with thoughts of what could have been a disastrous situation?

"Come here, baby" V said to Terri.

Terri got up and walked over to V to receive what they like to call a "20-second hug". This was just long enough to console, comfort or convince someone you really want to be with them.

"I'm sorry," V said.

"Thanks, baby…for breakfast, that is" Terri said.

"You're welcome. Say, where's Vas?"

"Still sleep. It's Saturday, you know."

"So? When I was young, we used to look forward to Saturday mornings. The cartoons! Man, those were the days!"

"Yeah, we…I mean, I did too. Loved them!"

"Well, these days, Saturdays aren't the same. I don't know what they play on TV now."

"Real estate shows; car auctions; fishing shows; shit like that," Terri said.

"That's bullshit. I sure hate it that Vas missed out on what we grew up on."

"Yeah. Let me go and get him so he can at least get some of this great breakfast, okay?" Terri asked.

"Sure. Go ahead."

"Watch your mouth, boy!"

"What!? What did I say wrong?"

"You called me a gore head. Don't be calling me no gore head!"

"Oh, real funny, chick! Ha!"

Terri left the kitchen headed towards their son's bedroom. V poured himself a cup of coffee and then looked out the window facing a frozen creek. He wondered why when it got cold, everything seemed to appear gray. He was happy, though. He was in need of nothing. He knew that at this moment of his life, things were pretty good.

CHAPTER 2

MAKE YOU TALK.

Jr. and Patricia were sitting on the side of their indoor heated pool at their 'gift' home. The very home that belonged to the famous or should it be said, infamous Victor Taylor and then inherited' to them by his brother Vincent. They had decided to take a swim before taking in some breakfast and maybe take a drive through the countryside. Saturdays can be lazy for some; or relaxing…depends on how you look at it. It was a cold morning and the sun hadn't come all the way up yet, but a cold morning never stopped swimming to be the norm. The pool was enclosed completely by glass that allowed them to see out but since they were gated and secluded, no one could see in…except the occasional critter…and they had to look hard to see.

"Is that a snow owl I hear?" Pat asked.

"Hell, I don't know. I don't know a snow owl from a snow plow. Ask me, and I'll tell you that owls were mainly down south. And how can you hear that anyway?" Jr. responded.

"I have good ears."

"No, you have some big ears! Ha ha!"

"Whatever. Well, if it isn't an owl, it must be a hawk out there this morning."

"There you go again!"

"What?" Pat asked.

"Using your FBI skills. Girl, you are too smart! Besides, I thought birds flew South for the Winter."

"Some do…some don't. Anyway, you're the one that's smart. Smartass!"

"Dumbo. Ha ha!" Jr. took pleasure in teasing his wife and she enjoyed returning the banter.

"Speaking of the FBI, you better be glad it's Saturday. You gotta fly to Louisiana on Monday" Pat said.

"Yeah, I know. I wonder why they didn't call on you to go. You were a better student than I was."

"I know." Pat said smugly.

"Shut up. Wait a minute. Maybe you weren't," Jr. said playfully.

"All I know is, when you get back, you better brief me on what's going on. Deal?" she said.

"Hell, naw, girl! No deal! I can't divulge my critical Intel to anyone and there is absolutely nothing you can do to me make me talk. I mean that!"

"Really?! You mean to tell me that there isn't **anything** that I could do to you to make you talk?"

"Uh…um…well, uh…maybe there is this one thing."

"This one thing, huh? What, pray tell, could that one thing be?"

"I'd rather not say. It is rather convincing."

"That's what I thought, punk."

"Punk?! Watch your tongue, Pat. You didn't call me a punk last night, now did you?"

"That's because you weren't a punk last night. My man showed up last night."

"Damn straight! And I'll show up each and every time I'm called upon…except for that one time."

"Yeah, don't remind me. Every time I think about that time, cooked spaghetti comes to mind. Ha ha!"

"Okay, make me feel bad, why don't you."

"Stop sulking, boy. It was only once and I'll give you this much; you had a lot on your mind. But, let me tell you this one thing for sure; don't for one second believe I can't get out of you what I want. You got that?"

"Yes, ma'am. Got it. Kick me, beat me, and make me write bad checks!"

Pat laughed. Jr. smiled. They enjoyed their home, each other and the time spent together.

* * *

More Wrongs: The Revenge

Victor Taylor packed the last of his clothes for his trip abroad. His new residence was now in Jamaica but he was preparing to fly to the United States. He had signed a contract that he believed required him to remain out of the United States for the rest of his life, but Victor had other plans. He had been gone long enough and in his mind, he deserved some revenue, some revenge and some restitution. He was going home… for specific reasons. He had cooled his jets for a minute, but the more he thought about what his brother, his mother, his father and his wife…at the time; did to him, they were fired right back up. The closer it came to catching his flight to the U. S., the more excited he got. He had a plan to hit them all where it hurt and he would be able to sit back and watch the show with joy.

"Damn, Vance, I can't believe it took over four years for you to get us back in the U. S.!"

"Don complain, bruddah. I did wot I had to do and so did you."

"I'm not complaining…I'm just saying. That sun had your ass baked! I think that's what took the longest."

"You know wot I had to do. I made all of de necessary arrangements, as well as took all of de reesks! I gave up a lot of ass for you, so, shut de hell up! I be helping **your** ass! Won't lie dough. If tings work out de way me plan, I be helping me own ass, too. I be entitled!"

"Well, you can kiss my ass, Vance. All of this preparation; all of this background shit; all your plans; they better work." He thought, *Besides, I have some plans of my own when we get back in.*"

Victor would not be travelling alone. He was arguing with his **other** brother…his triplet, Vancelot Taylor. He met him when he first involuntarily moved over to Jamaica. All he knew, all his life, was that he was a twin. He had no idea that he and Vincent were not just twins, but had **another** identical brother! Vance was the baby of the three, but he was not a novice. He was quite educated and Victor would find Vance to be quite instrumental in them returning to the United States. Identical triplets are a rare occurrence, but it is certainly possible and Victor, Vincent and Vancelot proved that. Victor was certain that V had no idea of this new situation in their lives, so Victor would make sure to use this to his advantage. Vancelot, or Vance as he liked to be called, had a plan to retrieve some of, if not all of the money due to Victor…and himself, as well, so these two brothers would be travelling companions and partners in crime. Even though, Victor was under the impression that he was not 'supposed' to return, there was nothing in the contract about Vance coming to America, because Vance was unknown to V and signed no contract. So, while Vance could and would boldly enter the U. S. of A, Victor had to 'sneak' in. But once in, it would be on!

"It weel work, if you don get too big for your breetches. I don know wot plans you be having, but don move until me tell you so. We don need no interruptions in de plans. D'yuh 'ere me?"

"Yeah, I hear you. We just better move fast. I want in and out before anyone even knows I was there!" he lied.

"I know. Me, too, bruddah. Me, too. Quick quick! Like a frumious Bandersnatch!"

"A what?! That's a damn fictional character in Alice in Wonderland! You're stupid."

Vance laughed. He was a bit surprised that Victor knew this bit of trivia.

Even though Vance looked exactly like his brothers, he had been a shade darker in his skin tone because of his location, so he and Victor couldn't go back until Vance could get his skin tone lightened. It took over four years of sacrificing not going to the beaches and hitting on tourists and taking them to his loft for a night of 'Jamaican fun', as he called it. He had to stay out of the sun, so Victor's personal valet, Dez did all of the running around for both brothers. Dez was paid well, so he didn't mind at all. But even with Vance staying out of the sun, it still wasn't enough. Victor had to hire a dermatologist to use laser skin lighteners for Vance until they were happy with the desired shade. All Vance had to do after that, was cut his hair, shave his face and perfect his English dialect. He thought it best to do that after they reached the states. He could get into the states a lot easier if he didn't have all the attributes of his brothers. His Jamaican dialect would even prove to be a plus. He would correct that after they got settled and started implementing his plans.

"Well, I'm all packed. You ready?" Victor asked.

"Why, yes, I am. You see, if we leave now, we can get into the U. S. in the wee hours of the morning and you know not many people will be expecting either one of us…especially not me. You still trust me, don't you?" Vance inquired.

"Yeah, I guess I do. Hey! What the hell happened to your accent? You sounded just **like** Vincent! Or me, for that matter."

"I've been practicing and it's time I put the island talk on the back burner for now. The more I talk like you and V, the less I'll mess up. Aw-ight? Of course, I'll use my home dialect while we fly, but I will be using this 'primitive' slang as much as possible."

"Damn, man, that's scary good!"

"I know, right? Boo!" Vance said as they walked out of the house.

CHAPTER 3

CAN'T STAY AWAY

Moms was putting the finishing touches on a strawberry pie she had baked. While she was admiring her work, she was interrupted by a man's voice.

"Well, hello, Ms. Taylor!"

Moms turned around suddenly to face a smiling Antony Sabino. "Huh? Oh, hey there, Mr. Sabino! You startled me."

Mr. Sabino was the known-by-everyone 'head gangster' in town. He wasn't into killing or robbing, but he was still respected as someone not to mess with. It turns out that Sabino was none other than Moms 'deceased' husband, Thomas Taylor, in disguise. His sons, Victor and Vincent found him out years ago and he even made a deal with the boys that he would either leave town or if he stayed, he would steer clear of Moms. He wound up doing neither.

"Sorry about that. Wasn't my intention, you know" Sabino said.

"Yeah, I know. I was just so wrapped up in this catering job, I didn't even hear you come in. It's not the biggest function I've done, but it doesn't matter to me. I want to do a good job every time!"

"Yeah, I know. I'm the same way. If it ain't damn near perfect, then why even put it out, right?"

"That's right!" Moms said. "There! All finished. What brings you over here, Mr. Sabino?"

"Look, how many times I gotta tell you? Call me Antony…or Tony… or 'Bino. Anything but **Mr.** Sabino. That was my dad's name. Ha ha!"

"Okay…Tony? What brings you all the way over here? I know it wasn't just to see me, was it?"

Sabino acted shy.

"Well, it is always nice to see you, Ms. Taylor. I realize you have your own business and I know your man isn't around anymore, so I like to help when I can. Besides, can't I come and view you sometimes?"

"View me? See there? Men won't act right."

"What? What did I do wrong?"

"You want me to call **you** something other than 'Mister', but you still call me 'Ms.' I have a name, too."

"Oh. Sorry. So, what should I call you? Moms? What is your name, anyway?"

"It's Elaine. Don't call me Moms. Call me Elaine. Not everyone can do that, you know?"

"Is that right? So, I must be special, huh?" he asked.

"Your fishing, Tony. I'm not saying you're special. I'm just saying what I said. Now, you were saying something about how nice it was to see me…or in your words, view me?" Moms was smiling by now.

"So, who's fishing now? I was just saying that it's always nice to see your pretty face."

"Okay, Mr. Flattermouth. That's enough. First you were fishing for a compliment, but now you're fishing for a catch! Careful. Your pole may not be strong enough to hold this one."

"My…uh…pole?"

"Okay…uh, that didn't come out the way I intended. Get your mind out of the gutter."

"Ha, hee, hee!" Sabino laughed.

"Yeah, that's funny. Stop laughing. Since you are here, you wanna help me load my truck with all this food instead of setting me up to say the wrong things?"

"I'd be glad to! What do you want me to put in first?"

"Put in? Oh, the truck." Moms was blushing now. She felt like all she could say led to the gutter. She would try to be careful with her words from now on.

"Grab those fruit trays, please."

"Okay." With that, Sabino grabbed one of the fruit trays and headed out the door to Mom's catering truck. Moms took notice at his movements.

"You know something, Tony?"

"Yeah?" Sabino whirled around to face Moms.

"I just noticed something. You remind me of my Thomas. Sorry, I don't mean to compare you two and I hope it doesn't offend. A little, that is. Little things you do."

"Really? Well, I'm not offended, but I'm going to have to work on that. Wouldn't want to make you feel bad thinking about him."

"Nope" Moms said. "Don't change a thing. I like it."

"So, I can keep wiggling my butt?"

Sabino grinned as he exited the shop. Moms blushed…and grinned, too.

* * *

"I wanna see Mammaw!"

Vasyl was restless and wanted to get out of the house. He was throwing a mini tantrum and it wasn't pretty. Vasyl. That's what Vincent and Terri named their son: Vasyl Edmond Taylor. Edmond was Terri's father's name and Vasyl was just another boys name that started with a V. Don't ask why. They don't even know. They did look up the meaning first and they wanted their son to have a name that would personify his character. He was born on Christmas Eve, so he was used to getting almost anything he wanted and Vasyl realized his birthday was just a couple of weeks away. He also realized being the only child around in this family won a lot of attention from everyone.

"We can't see Mammaw now. She's working today, Vas." Terri tried to explain.

"So. She can work if she wanna. I still wanna see her!"

"**Vas!**" Vas's father walked in and his booming voice kicked in. "You stop all that noise! You cannot see Mammaw today. We will try to see her tomorrow, okay?"

Vas calmed down at the sound of V's sternness. "Okay, Daddy. But, now you and Mama have to take me to the movies."

"What? Who says?" V asked.

"**I** say! That's who" the little boy responded.

"Boy! You don't talk to m…"

Terri interrupted.

"Okay, Vas. Go and get your coat."

"Yay!" Vas went running out the room to retrieve his jacket.

"Now why did you interrupt me? And why did you agree to that?" V asked.

"Come on, V. You know that was cute, right? Besides, it shouldn't bother you that your son likes spending time with the both of us…or does it?"

"Naw, it doesn't bother me. It's just that he can't have every damn thing he wants. We're the parents here. Not him and the one thing he will know in this household, is that Mama and Daddy make the rules. Are you okay with that?"

"Not only am I okay with it, it's kinda sexy! You being the man and shit."

"Good. Because if it isn't alright, then I may have to find someone else who likes it." V paused. "Sexy, huh?"

"Yep." Terri said with bedroom eyes.

"VAS! Come on, boy! Hurry your little butt up!"

V looked at Terri and smiled.

"Maybe we can catch an earlier matinee and then come back home and put his little ass to bed" V whispered to Terri.

She playfully bit his ear.

"I was thinking the same thing, Tiger!"

CHAPTER 4

NICE & FUN

"This is nice!" Lisa Vasquez was enjoying her wine, cheese and fruit with her fiancé, Chase Morton. She used to be Victor Taylor's secretary and then Vincent's; when he took over the firm. She still works at the firm, but she answers to Belinda Jett, who was promoted after V left. Chase used to be Victor's number one attorney and was called on to cover big cases that Victor didn't cover himself. He no longer worked there, but his relationship with Lisa grew. He decided to take her on an impromptu brunch at Jacques'. It was December and there was a little nip in the air. That wasn't exactly true…it was cold! That didn't stop Chase from being romantic. It was this same location just a year ago that he asked Lisa to be his wife. There was no better feeling in his mind when she said 'yes.' His plan now was to make her the happiest woman alive and maybe even one day, take her away from the position of 'administrative assistant'.

"Yes, it is" he replied, "but it wouldn't be half as nice if I wasn't with you. I never knew I could love someone as much as I love you."

"Aw. You are a smooth talker, Mr. Morton."

"Nah. You make it easy."

"Anyway, I want to talk to you about something.'"

"Not before you make amends."

"Amends? For what?"

"I just told you that I never knew I could love someone as much as I love you and all you did was compliment my ability to talk smooth."

"Oh, baby, I'm sorry. I love you more."

"Really? We'll see about that."

"I guess so. So, can we talk now?"

"Sure. What is it, baby?" Chase asked.

"I...uh...what I want to say is...uh."

"What's wrong, Lisa? Did I do something wrong?"

"Well, I wouldn't say 'wrong', just something I don't quite get. It is something you did, but I wouldn't say it was a wrong thing you did."

"Talk to me, baby. You can say whatever you want to me. Besides, if I did something, it couldn't have been wrong," he said playfully.

"Okay. Well...well, why did you give up your position at the firm? You were placed in charge and Victor trusted you to run the company and you left after a year. I just don't understand why you did that? Didn't you like what you were doing? You were certainly good at it, but then you knew that didn't you?"

Chase smiled and took a sip of wine before answering.

"Yeah, I was pretty good, wasn't I? I've always wondered why you haven't asked me this sooner, but I have my reasons."

"Are you going to tell me?"

"Sure. I left for two reasons. First of all, remember when we found out that after the firm was sold, it wasn't Victor Taylor who made that transaction, now was it? It was Vincent Taylor. He made some smart moves and there was nothing that Victor could do to stop it. So...since I wasn't actually Victor's choice to take over, I really didn't receive his blessings, right? I probably would have been had it been Victor, though. But let me tell you something; if Victor Taylor **ever** comes back into the picture, he's going to go cutthroat on everybody and anybody he feels gypped him and I wasn't going to be on his hate list. Just because I worked there and had his position, would have been enough for him to go after me."

"Okay, I'll give you that, but you know I still work there, right? So, what's the second reason?" Lisa asked with concern.

"You're a secretary, so it shouldn't affect you any. No offense. Then again, he would go after you to spite me."

"None taken," Lisa responded.

"Anyway, when V came into the money he did, he needed consultation and direction. I felt I would do better being his personal financial advisor than being an attorney that Victor would have a vendetta against. When people started finding out how good I was at this, I now have a slew of clients. Besides, I make a hell of a lot more money in my new position and I don't feel threatened."

"You're pretty sharp, Chase. I'll bet no one knew you had a law degree and an accounting degree. **That's** why everyone says you're so smart, huh?"

"Nah, the smartest thing I ever did was hook up with you."

Lisa blushed as she toasted with her man. She took a sip and smiled.

"You know what, Chase?"

"What's that, babe?"

"I like you, too!"

* * *

"Now, wasn't that fun!" Terri asked V. She, V and Vas, just left the movies and was headed to the dairy bar for some ice cream.

"Yeah, that was fun!" Vas answered before his father.

"She wasn't talking to you, boy. Man, he's so busy! I hate to admit it, but smart, too."

"Well, he's your son." Terri said.

"Oh, so I'm smart, too? Yeah, that was a fun time. Pretty good movie. Now it's time for that ice cream. Anybody ready for some ice cream?"

"Yay! Yes! **I** am! **I** am! I want Truchey Fruchey."

"Do you mean Tooty Fruity?" Terri asked her son.

"That's what I said. Ain't it Daddy?"

V could barely contain his laughter, but for the sake of his son's feelings, he bit his tongue.

"Yeah, son. That's exactly what you said. Let's get this treat so we can get home. Man, you can tell this boy is a native New Yorker, huh? Ice cream in the winter. Go figure."

"Well, after we get **that** treat, then you can get **this** treat, huh?" Terri whispered.

"Girl, if you're serving dessert, I'm partaking!" V whispered back.

CHAPTER 5

E. T. A.

Vance got off the plane with his dreads down and all over his face. He sported a Blackhawks jersey with black blue jeans. Victor wore a light brown fedora, put on gray fake sideburns, a much thicker salt and peppered fake moustache, light gray contact lenses and horn-ribbed bifocal glasses. He wore a tweed jacket with corduroy pants and a scarf wrapped tight around his neck. The brothers came into Newark Airport, just outside of New York City, with fake ID's. Victor was Professor Timothy Carr and Vance was Solomon Madden. Vance grabbed a scarf and put it around his nose, mouth and neck.

"See? That flight wasn't so bad, now was it? Less than 4 hours. Not bad, right, Professor Carr?" Vance asked Victor.

"I guess it wasn't that bad, Mr. Madden. Let's get our shit so we can get to the hotel, okay? I'm tired, man."

"Right. Me, too. But we won be sleeping too long on dis Sunday morning. We got items to pick up and we got to go over de plans one more a-gin."

"Hey! You're accent, dude!"

"Oops! Sorry boot dat. I did tell ya dat I would use it until me plans are on de way. Me have it corrected by tomorra."

"You better! Fuck this up if you want to! It **will** only be twins!"

"P'shue!" Vance made a sound with his mouth. He didn't fear Victor like others and he also felt he was the major cog in this wheel and Victor was a minor link that helped keep the motor running. Victor pulled out his cell phone and dialed.

"Who you calling, Professor?" Vance asked.

"Uber. Who did you think, dumbass?"

"Oh. Sorry. Damn, it's cold, here! I haven't even been outside yet and I can feel the chill in the air!"

"It's New York in the Winter, fool. But you're not sorry yet, brother. Just don't give me a reason to make you sorry, okay?"

"P'shue."

The brothers grabbed their bags and headed toward the front of the airport to wait on their ride. Small talk was made as they sat down inside looking out the glass windows.

"Well, I will say this much, Vance; you having us come in the states in the wee hours of the morning was pretty smart. It's people here, but not that many."

"I told you. When I found out what was going on, I started planning."

"Yeah, about that. How did you find out what was going on? You live in Jamaica. I know you have the internet, and you're a hacker, but this shit wasn't advertised."

"I will tell you. There is someone I befriended years ago. He came to the islands for a vacation and he thought I was you. It confused him because he had seen you earlier in court and not as dark-skinned as I was. But he thought it made since to darken some when swimming and enjoying Jamaica. That water and that sun will bake a person! Anyway, I told him some bullshit story of just happening to look like you. You know, everyone has a twin somewhere in this world, right? In this case, a triplet, right? Anyway, I helped him with some information that proved very progressive and financially advantageous. I actually started the ball rolling! He kept me abreast of what he was up to and when he needed some more advice or computer savvy, I would give it to him. Well, when everything popped off, I had already hacked into the system and knew it was ready before he did, and when it did, I was left out of the picture. I think he forgot about me. You know I was pissed, right? Anyway, how's my accent so far?"

"It's good, man. Really good. Go on, finish." Vic said.

"Okay. Thanks. So, I was cut out of the deal and I swore to myself that I would cut myself back in. All this time over there, I learned everything there was to know about computers, but I wanted to go further and that's where the hacking knowledge kicked in. I know how to get to the money, but I needed more resources. You can't just hack into a system, take money and the Feds not hunt you down. I needed your help like you needed mine…you just didn't know you needed my help. I couldn't do shit over in the islands, but now that it's you and me in the states, we're going to make this happen!"

Vance dropped his head in reflection.

"Yeah. I knew about the money and even though I could hack computers, I was not able to decrypt the codes to get what was mine. Can't believe that dude cut me out."

Victor started smiling and stared out into the morning darkness. In his mind, he had figured something out. Vance noticed.

"What are you smiling about?" Vance asked

"Your friend. Did he have a nickname? Would he be known as the Colonel?" V wanted to know, still smiling.

"Nah. His name was Casey. He had a great plan, but was missing some important info. His plan worked and I helped him pull it off. I just can't believe that fucker cut me out of the deal!"

"Casey? Kevin Casey?!" The smile left Vic's face.

"Yeah. What, you know him?"

"I'll just be shitted on" was all Victor could come up with. Their ride pulled up, they loaded the car and on were on their way to their temporary abode. At this point, Victor had nothing more to say...for now. Now, he was more pissed than before...and more determined.

* * *

Moms tossed and turned all night. She couldn't stop thinking about Mr. Antony Sabino.

"Tony. Boy, you crazy. I should say 'I'm crazy'! Why am I thinking about that Italian man? Come on, Elaine, pull yourself together. You DO NOT want to be with Antony Sabino. Do you? Lord, help."

She turned her lamp on beside her bed and reached into the top drawer of her nightstand. She pulled out a picture of Thomas Taylor, her late husband and sat up in the bed. She thought of how handsome he was.

"Now, this was a man! Woo wee, do I miss you! I wish you were here with me. I guess you know you have a grandchild, right? Cute little boy. Vincent's child. Imagine that, would you? They named that boy Vasyl. What Black parents do you know names their sons, Vasyl? Shocking, huh? I guess not for you. You can see everything that's going on, can't you? Well, if you can, will you tell me something; why am I falling for this other man?"

CHAPTER 6

NEW ORDER

Sunday came and went like any other Sunday. Moms, Terri and Vasyl went to church, while V stayed home and 'rested'. Vas was just happy to see his Mammaw and Moms was just as ecstatic as her grandchild. V had been going to church a lot more lately, but he didn't feel you needed to be in church every Sunday just to have a relationship with God. He turned on the TV to catch the Sports Reporters on ESPN so he could keep up with the football games that would be played this day. He thought he'd make a couple of bets, since he was on a lucky streak. He went to the fridge and grabbed a Henry's Hard Cider and headed back to the couch. No sooner than he sat down, his cell phone rang.

"Damnit. I left it plugged up in the bedroom" he said.

He ran down the hall to retrieve his phone, but it stopped ringing by the time he got to it. He looked at the screen and saw it was his best friend, Jr., so he called him back.

"Hey, man! What you doing?" Jr. asked.

"Nothing, dude. Fixing to watch some football, that's all. What's up?"

"What? No church, today?"

"Not today" V answered.

"God 'gon git you, boy!"

"Shut up. I ain't done nothing wrong. I sent my tithes; it's just that my body will be here at home."

"Uh, huh. Say, you know I've been called out of town, right?"

"Naw, I didn't know. When did you find out and what for?"

"They contacted me last week, but didn't say what for. I'm leaving in the morning. Just thought you wanted to hang out for a minute."

"Sure, dude. Where at? Here? There? Somewhere else?"

"Somewhere else. Let's get a steak and drink at Elaine's. What time is good for you? Now, don't make it too late. I have to spend some quality time with my woman, if you know what I mean?"

"Quality time, huh? What, you playing Uno with her or something? Ha ha!"

"Yeah, Uno. You're not funny and you know what I mean. What time, man?"

"What time is it now?" V said, looking at his watch. "It's 9 o'clock now. How about noon? The game will be on by then."

"That'll work. Want me to pick you up?"

"Yeah. No sense in me wasting up all my gas."

"Boy, you are so full of shit it's coming out your eyes. I'll see you at noon."

"Okay. I'll be ready. Oh, and by the way…you're paying for the steak."

"Bet. This time."

V hung up and went back to his spot on the couch.

Hell, next time, too, he thought to himself, smiling.

* * *

"Say, mon! Wake up, brudda! We got tings to do!"

Vance was shaking Victor out of a deep slumber. This pissed Victor off.

"Damn, man! **Sleep**!"

"I know you're sleep. Dat's why I wake your ass up! Come on, Vic! Let's get to dis!"

"There you go with that damn accent again. Fix that shit, aw-ight?"

"Later. Right now, we quine work."

"Shit!" Victor rolled out the bed and headed for the shower. After showering and shaving, he put on some khaki pants and a Thomas Dean button down shirt. He came out of the bathroom just as room service was leaving. As far as he was concerned, it was now time for Victor to take over this whole ordeal.

"I ordered us some breakfast, juice and coffee. Guine, eat up."

"Appreciate that, Vance" Victor said while taking a sip of coffee. He continued. "But we need to discuss a few things first."

"Okay. Make it quick quick. What up?" Vance said while stuffing his mouth with eggs.

"Well, you know how you have this plan to get what's ours, right? That's cool and all, but now that we are in the states, I am calling the shots from now on."

"Like hell, you call de damn shots! Wha de hell you talking aboot? Vance asked.

"What I'm talking about is, I will do what you need me to do to get that money. But you will do what I need you to do to help me get my revenge. I didn't come back here to just win and walk away. I came back to stomp ass and gloat!"

"Wha dýa won me doing? Me not be your flunky, boy!"

"Did I say you were my flunky? Naw, you're my brother, right? I'm helping you, ain't I?"

Vance nodded.

"Well, guess what? Your ass is going to help me, too. Besides, you might like what I have in store for you to do. It involves a female… and sex."

"So? Me can get me own female…have all me life…*and* sex!"

"I know you can but this will be so much more fun. You'll see. Besides, either you agree with me or we might as well get back on that goddamn plane. You tell me that what I got was chump change, but I had it pretty good over there in Jamaica. Hell, I was getting my fair share of booty, too you know. And money? Damn, son, I have no money problems. You see, the more I think about this, it appears to me that **you** want this money more than I do! Yeah, I was gypped, but I'm good! Now, you can get mad or you can scratch your ass and get glad."

Vance was steaming by now. He just thought he was in control. He was finding out different.

"Okay. Wha do me do for you?"

"First, you fix that damn accent right now. I mean it! If you use that 'island talk' one more time, I'm going to punch you in your throat. Understood?"

Vance nodded again, eyes glued on Victor. He had stopped eating by now.

"Next," Victor continued, while pulling out a piece of paper, "here is a list of things I...uh, we need to add to the list of things you need."

Vance looked over the list with disgust. He needed Victor, but now he was feeling used.

"So, we use your money to get all this, right?"

"Yeah, it's temporary. I'll get it back from you when this is all over."

"You're a bastard, you know dat?" Vance said.

"Hell, son. I thought you stayed abreast of what was going on. If you did like you say you did, you already knew I was a bastard! Now we kick this off tomorrow! Get your shopping shoes on, son!"

CHAPTER 7

Independence

V got up and got dressed. He didn't wear the usual business casual attire he always wore when going down to his new company. This time, he put on a pair of freshly starched blue jeans and a T-shirt that had the alligator on the front. He liked those. He felt that even if he wasn't sharp, he could at least be clean…and to some, it might have been considered sharp, as well. Terri was also getting dressed, but she wore a blue business suit with green pinstripes and a pair of Christian Louboutin pumps. She would be taking care of COC; which stands for Caught On Camera, Security Systems' day-to-day operations, while V would be helping Moms with a catering job. Vasyl would be staying with 'Aunt' Patricia, Jr.'s wife.

"Vas? You ready to go?" V called out to his son from the kitchen.

Terri entered the room, looking and smelling good.

"Why won't you let me help him get dressed?" she asked.

"I'm not stopping you. He does a pretty good job at three years old. Hell, might as well say four years old with his birthday coming up in a couple of weeks. It doesn't mean you're not his mother. I know, most kids that age need assistance. But Vas is special, and you know it. He's learning how to be independent, but I'm not taking you away from being his mother. He's got to learn to stay cool under any situation and make decisions for himself…even when it comes to clothes."

"I know. You're right. I'm just saying."

"I know, too. Watch this. Vas! Come on, son!" V called out.

"Coming!" came a little voice from outside the room. Vasyl came in the kitchen dressed in a matching Polo outfit with Air Jordans on his feet. He was cute, but he was sharp, too.

"See. Told you. With his cool ass." V said.

"Hmph. Too cute! You're almost as cute as he is, V."

"That's cool. I can live with that. You're beautiful. So there; compete with that!"

Terri smiled and blushed. She grabbed her keys and gave her boy a kiss on the cheek and her man a kiss on the lips before she headed out the door.

"See you later, V. Don't work too hard."

"Yeah, you neither."

"Oh, I won't. I'm only going to be there half a day. Just long enough to make sure everything is going smoothly. That's cool, isn't it, boss?"

"Yeah, that's cool. Just don't run any of my employees away and don't run my company into the ground, hear me?" V said jokingly. "I don't know how long I'll be with Moms but I'll come home as soon as I finish. Let me drop this boy off to Pat's and get Jr. to the airport."

"Wait! He hadn't eaten, yet."

"It's cool. I called Pat. She's got breakfast waiting for him."

"Oh, okay. Gotta run, lover. See ya! Oh, by the way, that orange juice was so good this morning!"

"Yep! It's the shit! See ya, later." V responded. He turned his attention to Vasyl.

"Well, my little man, are you ready to see Aunt Pat?"

"Yep."

"Yep?!"

"Yes, sir?"

"That's right. Yes, sir to men and yes ma'am to women. Got it?"

"Yes sir. Got it. Can we go now? I'm hungry."

"Yes sir. See how I did that? You're not a full-grown man, but you're a little man. Let me grab my keys and we are Audi."

As Vasyl and V step outside their house, the whirring and clicking sounds of a camera could be heard…not by them, but by the user. It had already been in use ever since V stepped outside his door to get the morning paper.

* * *

"Thanks for meeting with me, Warden. I know this was short notice."

Victor Taylor was shaking hands with Warden Pee Wee Bryant…now known as just Warden Bryant. **Victor** would now play the perpetration game…as V.

"No problem, V. What can I do for an old friend? You helped me when I needed you and I know you went through some shit in here years ago. Are you okay?"

"Just fine, Warden. Just fine."

"So, how's the wife and baby? Hell, he ain't no baby now, is he? What is he now, three…four?"

Victor didn't know. He had to think back to when he found out his 'wife' was pregnant with his brother's baby.

"Wife and baby? Yeah, he's going on four. They're good. So where is that security guard of yours…that racist redneck…uh, Cooper, right?"

"Oh, we transferred him to another facility. I didn't fire him, even though I wanted to. He and I didn't get along and when he found out that I was not a real prisoner and turned out to be his boss, he couldn't handle it. He kept jumping at any little thing that happened. It's like he expected something bad to happen to him or something."

"I see. Well, what about Casey?"

"Kevin Casey? Hell, he up and quit. Told the old Warden to shove it up his ass. Ha!"

"Quit, huh? Do you know where he is now?"

"Disappeared off the face of the earth. Nope. Haven't a clue."

"Oh, okay. So, is Big Percy still in?"

"Where else would he be? He's serving a triple life sentence and he sure isn't going to be transferred so he can have it better than he has it right now. Why do you ask?"

"Well, that's why I came here…to see him. You know we were cellmates, right? Do you think I could meet with him somewhere discretely?" Victor asked.

"V, I wouldn't be in this position today if it weren't for you, so sure! I can make that happen. Anything else you need?"

"No, that would be cool. Thanks, Pee Wee."

"Um…no one calls me that anymore. I don't allow it."

"Sorry about that. Didn't know. Thought I'd try it, though. Hee hee."

"Hee hee, hell! Anyway, now you know."

"Yes, I do. So…. about that meeting?"

"Oh, yes. Let me set this up for you."

"Thank you…Warden."

CHAPTER 8

SHOT CALLER

"So, did you get the pictures?" Victor asked Vance.

"Yes."

"And you did your shopping, right? The cars; the clothes; the surveillance camera? You got the other room and hooked it up?"

"I'm on top of everything you wanted me to be."

"Cool! So, Vance, my brother, are you ready to go out later tonight and pick up a chick?"

"Yes, I am. But not just any chick. This lady will have to be classy… and fine. Hell, I might even ask if she's had all of her shots. Shit, at this point, I'm the whore! So, did you talk to that guy in prison?" Vance inquired.

"Oh, yes. Big Percy. I didn't know he was a computer whiz and I spent a few weeks in jail with him when V switched places with me. He never mentioned it. He had a lot to do with the transactions that Casey put together. He's gay, though."

"I knew he was a computer whiz. And what does being gay have to do with anything?"

"Nothing. Just thought you'd want to know."

"It doesn't matter to me. He's not my boyfriend. He's just one of the missing pieces to our puzzle. Now tomorrow, you have to add another piece. You know that, right?"

"Man, I'm all over this. I'll handle my part; you just handle yours. By the way, were you able to make that call to V?" Victor asked.

"Yeah, but it wasn't me. I had to pay someone else to do the talking and convince him to move. V fell for it, though. He left your mother high and dry just to go help someone."

"**My** mother? She's your mother, too!"

"She may be my mother, but she ain't my mama" Vance replied.

"Okay, I get that and it's cool. Hell, if we play our cards right, we could be out of here in a couple of days."

"Shiiit. It's gonna take longer than that. That money won't transfer for a couple of days. A couple of weeks, maybe."

Vance was lying. He knew that as soon as he could punch the numbers he needed and have the signature he needed, the money would transfer immediately. It was just that Vance had never been out of Jamaica for anything, and he wanted to explore the states a bit more before returning.

"Damn, that long? Our plans might be discovered by then," Victor said.

"It won't matter if they are. I made all the arrangements. Don't forget; this was my idea."

"Okay. I'm going to let you get ready for this evening. I'm going to bed."

"Oh, you get to sleep and I have to stay out all night?"

"Looks that way" Victor said, while heading for the bedroom. "See you in the morning…'Victor,' Victor said to Vance.

"Bastard." Vance said while heading towards the shower.

"Oh, and Vance? Don't forget to get that shit down and to me ASAP." Victor said.

* * *

Vance walked into the nightclub. He decided on Cookie's, a quaint little jazz club, not too far from where he had his room. He figured if he were going to pick up someone, she had to have a little class about her, and in his mind, a woman that likes jazz instead of rap, was classy to him. There was nothing wrong with rap music…or country music…or classical music…or even a person that liked any of these. This was just Vance's personal opinion. Back home, he didn't care what they liked, since he was all about sexing. Most were visitors and tourists, so he would have his way with them and then send them on their way, but this was different. He was on their turf and if he hooks up with a girl tonight, she would have to fit some certain criteria. He had shaven and gotten a haircut that day. He had pictures of V to refer to and now the triplets were absolutely identical. It crushed him to have his dreadlocks cut off, but for the sake of the team…and the money, he did it. He had on a black Versace suit, with an embossed light gold imprint design. He wore a gold cravat and his socks were gold and black argyle print. He made sure he smelled good, so he went Versace all the way. He looked like he had a little money, which was the appearance he tried to exude. Truth is, he did have some money…a lot, to be honest…just not at his present disposal. Of course, Victor put a roll in his hand before he left the hotel room. As he perused the area, his eyes were immediately transfixed on the back side of a woman at the bar.

"Damn! If she looks as good from the front, then my search is over!" he said to himself. *Hell, this is happening faster than I thought*, he thought.

This lady who he was fixated on, grabbed her drink and then went to sit down at a table by herself. She wore a light blue satin blouse with black pants that had a blue logo of a tiger down one side of her leg. The high stiletto shoes she wore made her appear taller than she was and made her butt muscles flex. When she turned around, Vance noticed how gorgeous she was from the front and the style that made her stand out from anyone else there. The glitter found in her makeup, flashed like stars. Her dark-skinned tone was sexy to Vance. She was absolutely captivating! He couldn't help but wonder, though why she was all alone. It still proved to his advantage.

Perfect, Vance thought. He stood back and watched her walk across the floor to her table. After she took her seat, he moved towards her.

"Excuse me, Miss. Are you here with someone?" he asked.

"Maybe. Maybe not. Why do you ask?"

"I was wondering if maybe I could join you?"

"Sure. I mean, I guess so until my man shows up, that is. I'm not so sure you can afford me, anyway."

"Whoa. Maybe I shouldn't sit down. I don't want no beef with any man. And I can't afford you? Are you a prostitute? Vance asked.

"No, but I am high-maintenance. And don't worry, I was just kidding about the man. Sit down, buy me a drink."

"Hell, I just thought you might like some company, that's all."

"Oh, is that all?"

"I mean, I'll buy you a drink and we can talk…for now anyway" he said, smiling. "Who knows what else?"

Vance sat down and started bobbing his head to the live music that was playing. It was a group called Complete and they sounded good! They happened to be playing a song with some island flavor to it, so Vance was really enjoying it. Before Vance could strike up more of a conversation, the woman lit into him.

"Where have you been, you bastard?" the lady asked Vance.

"Huh? What do you mean?"

"I mean, where the hell have you been, Victor? It's been years since I've seen you. Did you leave the country or what?"

*Damn! She thinks I'm **Victor** and he should know her!*

"Oh. I've been away." Vance forgot that many of the people in this town knew Victor Taylor and he had surely been with many ladies and **this** particular woman knew Victor Taylor quite well, it seemed.

"Away? Hmph!" she said.

"I'm here now. That's all that matters, shouldn't it be?"

"I guess. I just didn't like the way you left me when you did. I guess I thought I was special to you, but I found out I'm not. I should be mad. For some strange reason, I'm not. You left me something…hell, that's better than nothing at all. I've been fine, thanks for asking. Got some great modeling gigs, so I'm doing alright. I guess time heals all wounds, huh? You've changed, though. Not as cocky or something."

"Well, change can be good sometimes, right?"

"It can, I guess. So…how's that baby of yours…and wifey, huh? I really don't want to know all that shit. How are you, Victor?"

"Look sweetheart, I didn't come here to answer questions. Now, we could sit here, drink drinks, listen to music and talk all night, but honestly, is that what you want to do with Victor Taylor? Don't you want this? Let's go somewhere…or should I say, to my place down the street? We could talk, listen to music, drink or…whatever while there."

"Down the street? When did you…you know what? Never mind. You have places everywhere, don't you? Why not my place?"

"Because, **I** call the shots, that's why."

"Damn, maybe I was wrong about you but it's that cocky shit I like and that's the Victor I'm used to! Let's go. You driving, right?" she asked.

"Nah. Took Uber. You driving?"

"Yeah, this time I am. Where we going?"

"It's not far. Just hand me the keys and strap yourself in, okay?"

"Okay. And Victor?"

"Yeah, sweetie."

"You gonna do me right tonight, aren't you? You're gonna make it up to me, aren't you?"

"You bet your sweet fine ass, I am!"

"All right, then! Home, James" she said jokingly, handing him her keys. She winked at the bartender as she left and he winked back. They both knew what was about to happen.

* * *

"So, how was the catering job with Moms today?" Terri asked V as they prepared to go to sleep. Vas was already sleeping. Pat tuckered him out…and herself as well.

"Oh, it went well. There were a lot of people there. Moms is good! That's all I can say."

V didn't want to go into too much detail as to how the party went: He knew he didn't stay long enough to know. Since he had asked Terri to fill in for him at his company, he didn't want her to feel used. The phone call he received earlier was from an old classmate of his…a fine, female classmate that V had a crush on. She was in a class one grade higher than him and he would have loved to have been with her. He just thought that she was out of his league. Hell, she thought the same thing at the time. I guess she missed out, V thought. Even though, V was loyally married to Terri, this particular woman **still** looked incredible! She had some car trouble and didn't know of anyone else to call…so she said. V knew he would never sleep around on Terri, but it didn't stop him from helping a friend…even if he **did** have feelings for her a long time ago…but that was a long time ago, and his attentions were on the love of his life; his wife, Terri. He vowed he'd never be like his brother, but he didn't like not telling Terri everything, either. Even though it wasn't cheating, it was still not being totally transparent and that, he knew, could get a person in trouble. He didn't want to leave Moms in a bunch, but he didn't want to leave a friend in trouble, either. He didn't even tell Moms why he was leaving; afraid of the judgment. Moms assured him she could cover it, but what Moms didn't tell V, was that she was going to call on Sabino to help, knowing he would come right over. V never made it back, so V never knew about Sabino or how it went.

"Well, that's good. I'm sure Moms was glad to have your help." Terri yawned.

"Yeah, she was. So how was your day? Anything I need to know?"

Terri mumbled something and fell off to sleep…just like that. Terri was too used to not having to work for a living. Sure, she had a law degree, just like Victor, and when she was married to him, she didn't work at all. But now that she was married to Vincent, there would be times when she would fill in for her husband, and it usually wore her out. No, neither V nor Terri really had to work, but V had a sense of respectability and pride owning his own business. V kissed her on the forehead. He was actually relieved she couldn't hold a conversation at the moment. He closed his eyes and followed his wife to Slumber land.

Don't you keep this to yourself…she needs to know, he thought.

CHAPTER 9

ARE YOU CRAZY?

"Hey, love!" said Jr.
"Hey, sugar! How was your flight?" Pat asked.
Jr. called his wife to catch her up on the current situation.
"Oh, the flight was fine. Got here about noon and sat in a briefing room until this evening. Funny thing, though."
"What's that?"
"They never did tell us why we had been called in. They said that they were still waiting on two other agents to make it in before they broke everything down."
"So how long are they talking about keeping you down there?"
"Hell, I don't know. They really didn't say. Could be a week, two weeks, maybe even a month! I told them I needed to get back home by Christmas to be with my wife. They laughed at me."
"Really? Damn! That sounds serious. So, when you do come back, what say we start talking about working on a family? Keeping Vas has got me to thinking I want a child of my own. How do you feel about that?"
"What do you mean, 'how do I feel'? It's your body."
"That's not what I meant and you know it. How do you feel about a child?"
"Honestly, Pat, I'm not that crazy about the idea. Don't get me wrong, I would love to have a baby with you. I just don't think that now is a good time. We're still young. Can it wait?"
"We're not that young, Jr."
"We're not that old, neither!"
Pat got quiet.
"Pat? You still there?"

"Yeah."

"You got quiet on me."

"Yeah."

"I'm sorry if I upset you, babe. How about we talk about this when I get back home? That might give me time to mull it over. Okay?"

"Yeah."

"Pat..."

"Look, I gotta go. I'll talk with you later. Call me tomorrow, okay? Love you."

"I love you, too, baby. Pat? Don't be mad at me, okay?"

"Yeah. I'm not mad. Bye, bae."

With that, Pat hung up the phone. She wasn't mad. Hurt? Yeah.

* * *

V was up earlier than usual. He didn't want to wake Terri or Vasyl. He felt he would make it up to Terri by having a long productive day at his company, even though Terri was none the wiser of his 'unfaithfulness'. He didn't do anything wrong, but in his mind, he didn't do everything he was supposed to do, either.

I should have told her, he thought to himself. *I'll do it this evening. At least a whole day would have gone by and I would have worked. Besides, she shouldn't be **too** upset. I hope not, anyway.*

He stepped outside to grab the paper so that when Terri and Vas woke up, they wouldn't have to go outside. He had actually done this every morning he and Terri had been together. No matter where they were located together, he would always retrieve the paper. It was cold anyway and the weather forecast called for snow. 20% chance, but a chance nonetheless. While he was outside, he stood and looked up to the sky for a minute, thinking of how lucky he was to have Terri in his life.

"If you listen to sinners, Lord..., thank you" he said towards the sky.

He went back in, poured him a cup of coffee to go in a sealed container; the kind that keeps coffee hot most of the day, and then left a lovely card on his pillow right next to Terri. He had bought quite a few love cards and filed them away to use on any occasion. When you're rich, **everyday** can be a holiday or a special occasion and V would leave a card for Terri when she least expected it. This was just one of the things that kept their love life fresh and exciting. He didn't kiss her on the forehead, in fear of waking her. He grabbed his keys, his coffee and his coat and he was on his way to work. The only thing was, he was not the only one working. The whirring and clicking of that camera was operating on overtime as he sped off down the highway.

* * *

"Okay. Is he gone?" Victor asked.

"Yeah, I think so." Vance paused, waiting for confirmation and a delivery. "Yeah, he's gone." Vance answered

"Cool, send me the pics. I'm sitting outside the men's store now waiting on them to open."

"I'm not. I'm back at the hotel."

"At the hotel? How the hell are you getting the pictures we need?" Vic asked.

"Don't you worry about that. Just be glad to get them."

"Alrighty, then. Oh, by the way, how did last night go for you?"

Vance just smiled as he answered.

"It went better than well!"

"So, you hit that?"

"Yes sir, I did. She thought I was you! Hate to admit it, but that helped."

"Hell yeah, it helped! You were the great Victor Taylor! So, did you get the video?"

"I have it with me" Vance assured Victor.

"Did you change clothes like planned?"

"Look, Vic! I'm not stupid! I did everything you told me to do! Damn!"

"Did she ask you why you were changing clothes?" Vic asked.

"Damnit, Vic! She thought I was you, remember? She probably knew not to ask!"

"Hey, I'm just making sure. I don't need any slip ups. Dig?"

"Okay, okay. Yeah, I got the video and I took a selfie of me with her... with my changed clothes."

"Yeah? Send it to me now. I wanna see."

Vance pulled the phone down from his ear and went to his gallery. He texted the pictures he received from this morning and the selfie from last night over to Victor.

"I just sent it."

"Got it. Now I know how to dress for today."

Victor looked at the pictures and his mouth fell open.

"Oh, **shit!** This is perfect! You **hit** this, right?"

"I beat it up like it stole something."

"Did she ever say her name?"

"Yeah. I made her. Why? You do know her, don't you?"

"Hell, yeah, I know her. I'm just trying to see what name she told you. Who did she say she was?"

"She said Carrissa. No, wait…it was Cassandra…Cassie for short." Victor couldn't do anything but laugh. He laughed until he cried. His plan was coming together even better than he thought it would.

"Send me her number…just in case," Victor said, still laughing.

"What's wrong with you Victor…you crazy or something?"

"Man, I am past crazy! I'm delirious!"

CHAPTER 10

VISITATIONS

V was straightening up his desk at his company. His office was closed off from his employees, but it was glass all around, so they could see him working…or not. He felt it was a good move to allow them to view his dealings and know that if he were working, then they should be working, too. The security system business was quite profitable, even if V did have to compete with other companies. Since he had a few people in his corner who knew a little something about protecting a home; Big Percy; Warden Bryant; the Colonel; he was able to replace quite a few accounts owned by other companies, as well as obtain brand new customers. His company was growing and he was considering franchising it. He picked up his phone and called a major real estate company who was building new offices all over the city. He was determined to get this account.

"Hello. Dick? Hey, this is Vincent Taylor with COC Security Services. How are you doing? (pause) That's great, man! Say, I was wondering if you are still considering using us for your security needs. (pause) Yeah. You should have received those numbers yesterday."

"Mr. Taylor?" a woman's voice spoke over the desk intercom.

"Hold on a minute, Dick." He punched a hold button; then a button on the intercom. "Yeah, Karen."

"Mr. Sabino is here to see you."

"Sabino? Okay, send him in." Two punches once again, in reverse order. "Yeah, Dick, I'm back. Oh, you found them?"

V motioned for Sabino to come in. Sabino came in the office, closed the door behind him and sat down in the chair in front of the desk.

"So, it sounds like we **can** do business? Cool! I'll fax the contract over and when you sign it you can fax it back, okay? Ok, talk to you later. Yeah, technology has surely made things easier. Bye." V hung up the phone and turned his attention to Sabino.

"What the hell are you still doing in town?" V asked Sabino.

"Now, is that any way to speak to your 'old man'?" Sabino inquired in return.

"It could be. But no, not respectively. What's up, Dad?"

"Hey, son. Nothing much. Well…"

"Well, what? I guess since you're still around as 'Sabino', you're not hanging around Moms much, right?"

"Well…when can I see that grandson of mine?"

"Dad? You're seeing her, aren't you? Damn it, we agreed! Either you leave or if you stayed, you would **not** be seeing Moms. Am I right or wrong?"

"You're right…sort of."

"Sort of?"

"Yeah. Sort of. You wanted me to stay away, but you forgot about two things: one is I'm a grown-ass man and two, I'm your Father…you're not mine!"

V got up from his seat, reached across the desk and grabbed his father by his collars. Sabino just smiled.

"You know, you might want to rethink what you're doing right now," Sabino said. "How do you think this looks to your employees out there? They know who I am and it would look strange if I didn't retaliate against something like this. So…, you might want to show them true remorse for what you are doing. Let me go, brush me off and apologize. Apologize so much, that it looks like you're begging me not to hurt you or yours."

V loosened his grip, walked around the desk and went through the motions of appearing to apologize. He whispered in Sabino's ear.

"Bastard."

"Yeah, I love you, too son" Sabino whispered back. "That's better. Now sit down. We have to talk."

V went back around to his side of the desk and took a seat.

"Okay," V said, "I'm sitting. What do we have to talk about?"

"You know that guy that was in prison with you…Big Percy?"

"Yeah, what about him?"

"He's dead."

"Dead?!"

"Yep. Poisoned."

"Poisoned? Do they know who did it?"

"Well, the Warden had a talk with me last night. Seems that you were the last one to see him. You do know how this looks, right? Yesterday, was it?"

"I haven't seen Big Percy since last year! Who said I was at the prison yesterday?"

"The Warden. You met with him first. He allowed you to talk with him."

"Dad, I only go back to that prison every January after Christmas. I visit them and take them shit. Now it's December and I'm telling you, I was not there yesterday. Damn, I thought I was finished with this being accused of doing shit I didn't do!"

"Well, this does cast a shadow of doubt on you. You could have been the main person of interest, but the Warden said that anyone in prison could have done it. I told him that that was probably the best way to look at it. Hell, if you were there, you wouldn't kill anyone. I'm right about that, ain't I? I would think you spent all the time in jail you wanted…or didn't want."

"Damn right."

"So, if it wasn't you, V, then who was it? Victor?"

V just stared out as if he was looking straight through Sabino. His mind wandered to what might have happened. He put his head on his arms.

"V?" Sabino asked.

"Yeah," V answered with his head still down.

"You okay?"

V raised his head slowly and looked into Sabino's eyes; his father's eyes.

"Could've been. Vic's back. I just know it!" V said.

"Oh, shit," said Sabino.

* * *

Pat was wiping down her kitchen. She didn't realize how messy it could become fooling with Vas. She didn't mind, though. She just didn't realize the mess that was made, when it was being made. While she was working, she got a beep from the front gate. She looked at the monitor.

"V? What are you doing here? I thought you were working today?"

"Hey, girl! Let me in. I need to get something I left in the office."

"Okay." Pat buzzed him in.

This man told the truth. He really did need to retrieve something. There was only one problem. This was not V.

CHAPTER 11

I CAN PERPETRATE, TOO!

Pat opened the door to her home and hugged who she thought was V.

"Boy. What's up with you? I talked to Jr. last night!"

"Yeah?" Victor said, while heading to the office.

"Yeah, he's fine. Thanks for asking."

"Oh...sorry about that. Sort of preoccupied. This work shit, you know."

"Yeah. Well, I used to know. I'm still FBI, you know, but it seems like the bureau is shutting me out."

"FBI, huh?"

"You already knew that, V. Stop tripping!"

"You're right, I'm tripping." Victor reached the office and started looking around the room for **anything** that would have this girl's name on it. He met her at his brother's birthday party four years ago, but he could not remember her name. He picked up an envelope on the desk that gave him what he needed. Voila'!

"Look, Patricia, I have to get back to work, but I'm looking for something I left over here the other day and what I have to look for will take some discretion."

"This is my house, son! But then again, you did give it to me. I **guess** I can let you have your privacy. Holler at me before you leave, okay? I'll be in the kitchen. By the way, it isn't Playboy or some other porn shit, is it?"

"Naw, girl. I'll holla before I leave."

Pat left and closed the door behind her.

"Damn, she smelled good!" Victor said about Patricia.

Victor moved quickly, secretly hoping that no one had already found what he was looking for. He grabbed the step ladder and climbed up to a statue of Aristotle on the top shelf. He pushed a button on the bottom of the statue and it opened up from the belly. Inside was a state-or-the-art recording device that could hold a terabyte of video and audio footage. It produced clear, concise pictures with remarkable sound.

"Damn skippy!" Victor said.

He closed the statue and placed it back on the shelf. Before he left the room, he looked around for anything else that he could use for leverage. There was nothing worth taking, so he left something instead; a little friend called 'Bat'. He then made his way out. He headed for the front door instead of the kitchen.

"Say, Patricia!" he called out, "I'm leaving. You can come lock your door. See ya!" *I told you I'd holla at you*, he thought.

Victor got in 'his' car before Pat could make it to him. He had Vance purchase two cars that were identical to the one that V was driving. The tricky part was not to be driving around at the exact same time, in the exact same area. This was just in case the brothers had to be somewhere that required the ruse of being Vincent. Victor drove down the road until he came to his next destination. It was a house between V's and Pat's house. Victor had purchased it long before he was contracted to leave the states. No one lived there. It was just one of the homes Victor would use to have his flings in and he wouldn't have to be too far from his 'family' home…which was now Patricia and Jr's home. It had been over four years since anyone had been there so it needed dusting and cleaning, but he would have to tend to that later. He went inside and went straight to his studio. What people did not know about Victor Taylor, was that even though he practiced law, he dabbled a bit in music, as well. He had some nice tracks, but he never shared them with anyone. Fear of rejection kept him from it. He took the video recording he'd just gotten from Pat's place and placed it into his player to see what was on the tape. He sat and watched. The best thing about this technology was that all he had to do was punch in a date and the video would come up to the point he desired. The date was easy to remember…it was his birthday, March 19, 2016. When he found what he was looking for, he recorded that particular incident onto another disc. Now it was time to record what Vance had given him. He wound up listening to one of the tracks he laid down and nodded. *I might have to rethink this shit. That's pretty good,* he thought.

He then locked up his place and headed down the road again. He was on a mission and he wanted to hurt people quickly. With that being said, he headed to the hotel where he and Vance where residing.

"Vance! Where are you?" Victor asked as he walked through the door.

"In here, watching Classic TV. The Beverly Hillbillies is a funny show, you know?"

"Yeah, I know. I just don't watch a lot of TV. Well, except on the islands. Get up. Got a job for you" Victor said.

"What now?"

"Do you think you can hook up with Cassie? I mean, right now?"

"Yeah, I think so. Probably. Why?"

"Here put this on and give her a call to meet you ASAP." Victor handed Vance some clothes in a clear plastic covering.

"Isn't this the same outfit you're wearing right now?"

"It is. It's also the same outfit that V is wearing right now, as well. Let me ask you something else…you're a hacker, right?"

"It is what I am known for, yes."

"Can you hack into phone numbers and shit?"

"When it comes to a computer or wireless technology, there's not much I can't do!"

"Good. Here's what I need."

CHAPTER 12

SOLD!

Sabino sat in his chair at his factory. He was still in the business of producing 'Ghost', the product that made everyone so rich. Since no one was the wiser, except for a couple of FBI agents who happened to benefit from this, namely, Patricia and Jr., there was no reason to worry about being revealed. But his concern was not on his business; it was on his son, V. Sabino, who was really Thomas Taylor, thought back to when his boys were born.

"Mr. Taylor?" the Doctor said while walking up to him in the waiting room.

"Yes. I'm Mr. Taylor. Is everything okay?"

"Hi, I'm Doctor Evans. Everything's fine. Your wife is resting and your boys are healthy."

"Good. Is that all? Can I see them?"

"Yes, but first I need to discuss something with you."

"All right."

"Mr. Taylor, I don't want to alarm you, but it seems we have made a mistake with this pregnancy."

"What kind of mistake? My wife was pregnant and she had twins. Right? You just said everyone was fine."

"They are. But that's the problem. Your wife didn't have twins."

"What? She lost one? I thought you said boys!"

"I did. She didn't lose anything. She had triplets."

"Triplets?! How is that possible?"

"Well, it seems when we did the ultrasound, we could only detect two heartbeats. The last one must have been hiding."

"You're bullshitting me, aren't you? Is this some kind of prank?" Thomas asked.

"No sir. It's not often, but like I said, we made a mistake. You are the father of identical triplets. Some people think that's rare, but it's not. I don't know if they will grow up and look just alike, but for now, without a name tag on them, we can't tell them apart!"

"So, you put name tags on my sons? How? I wasn't there to name them. Does Elaine know?"

"Your wife? No, she doesn't. We had to sedate her during the delivery. We really didn't give them names, per se, but we had to do something, so as they came out, we labeled them "A", "B" and "C". Did you and your wife discuss names?"

"Yes. Victor and Vincent."

"Well, you need to come and put those names on who you want them to belong to. Oh, and you need to come up with another name, as well."

"Damn, we hadn't figured on three children. I don't know what to do."

"Do you want to see your sons? Your wife is still asleep and you can see her a little later."

"Yes. Yes, can you take me to them?"

As the Doctor and Thomas Taylor walked down the hall to where the babies were, Thomas was a bundle of emotions. Fear. Dread. Indecision. He knew he and his wife were just barely making it by themselves and bringing two additional people into the picture was going to make it hard on Thomas. But three? Thomas thought that he would not be able to give his family what they needed and he didn't want to be like his father and just leave when it got too hard. He was at a loss in what to do. He didn't know if Elaine Taylor would be excited to have three boys or would she be as afraid as he was right now. All the time, she thought it was two with extra kicking, when all along, it was really three. The last thing he wanted to do was put any more stress and strain on his wife. She had just carried his babies to term and she was tired. Now, he understood why. As they came to the window where the babies were on 'display', he looked at Baby A, Baby B and Baby C and even though they were perfect in his eyes, he was flooded with worry and trepidation.

"Which one was born first? Is it alphabetical?" Thomas asked.

"Yes, in that order."

"Okay, Baby A will be named Victor. Baby B will be called Vincent. And Baby C…" His voice trailed off, thinking of a name.

"Yes?" the doctor asked.

"I'm thinking… okay, let's name him Vancelot."

"Okay, I'll inform the nurses. Congratulations, Mr. Taylor!"

The doctor began to walk away when Thomas called him back.

"Doctor Evans? Can I talk to you for a minute?"

The doctor turned around and came up to Thomas.

"Sure. What is it, Mr. Taylor?"

"I'm…not so sure…that I want my wife to know about that third child."

"What?! What are you saying?"

"Hell, I don't know. I want the best for my family, but I know we would all suffer if it was five of us. I hate this feeling I have, but Elaine does not need to know…does she?"

The doctor looked at Thomas with concern. He paused before answering.

"Hold on a second" the doctor said, while pulling out his phone and making a call. He walked out of earshot of Thomas and spoke with someone for a couple of minutes. "Okay" was all that could be heard from the conversation before he hung up.

"Mr. Taylor, this is the most difficult and the strangest situation I have ever faced in my thirty years in this profession. Everyone has always wanted to keep their children, no matter how many. This might be a strange proposition to you, as well. My wife and I have always wanted children and well, she has not been able to make it through a pregnancy. She's lost two in our time together and it's been hard and painful. Of course, we're too old to have children now and we thought about adopting before, but at the time, she just couldn't get over losing those babies before they were born. We haven't talked about it in a long time, but now… Well, it seems that now we're ready, but if it's all the same to you, and I know you need to do this quickly, we can help each other out. I'm getting ready to retire and move to Jamaica; this month to be exact. I talked to my wife and she's willing to compensate you for the baby. I promise you, we will give him the best of everything, and you can even keep in touch. You can refuse us and risk your wife finding out you have three more mouths to feed or we could help each other. My wife is on her way up here right now to retrieve our little package and I

46

will transfer $100,000 to any account you tell me. You will have fewer financial worries, we'll make sure your wife never knows and my wife and I will have a child without going through all the rigmaroles of the system, as well as us facing the threat of being denied. So, what do you say?"

Thomas looked at his feet and thought.

"Mr. Taylor, you need to make a decision quickly before your wife wakes up and wants to see her babies."

Thomas looked up with a tear running down his face.

"Did you say $100,000?"

"Yes, I did."

"Well…can you make it 2?"

Sabino came back from his daydreaming to reality. He knew what he needed to do.

"Hell, I wonder what would be happening if all three of those boys were involved in this shit. Victor is vicious and who knows what plans he's cooking up. I know what to do. He told me not to bother him if I can help it, but it's time I called on the 'Big Dog'."

CHAPTER 13

Bearing Gifts

Victor reached V's new home, pretending to be his brother. He pulled up to the house but the one thing he hadn't figured into the equation was the fact he did not have a fob to open the garage door. He was thankful that Vance had done his homework. Finding out where V was living wasn't easy. This had a lot to do with the time Vance and Vic spent on the island, as well. V was travelling a lot with his new-found wealth…and woman, so it took a minute to locate him. It wasn't until he settled into one location, that Vance was able to find him. One thing about the Taylor boys: if they were faced with a situation unplanned, they would improvise, so, Victor parked in the circular driveway and honked his horn.

"V? What are you doing home?" Terri asked, as she opened the front door.

"What? I can't come home to see my beautiful wife?" Victor asked.

"Sure, you can. I thought you would be at work, that's all."

"Oh, I'm working, all right."

"How come you didn't park in the garage?"

"I'm not staying long."

"Well, how come you didn't use your key to come in?"

"Damn, Terri! Why all the questions? I'm home. Isn't that good enough?"

"Don't you 'damn' me, V. I can ask what I want."

"Okay. Sorry about that."

"Yeah. So, what's up?" Terri asked another question.

"Nothing. Just thought I'd come by for a little afternoon delight, if you know what I mean."

They went inside the house and closed the door behind them. Victor grabbed her by the hand and motioned his head to another room. He didn't know where the bedroom was, so he hoped Terri would lead him. She did. When they reached the bedroom, Victor held Terri close in his arms and kissed her deeply. After the kiss, Terri spoke.

"You know, that orange juice I had was pretty good this morning."

"Yeah, that's nice" Victor said, while kissing her on the neck.

"Hold on for a second, V. I have to check something in the oven. I'll be right back, okay?"

"Okay. I'll be right here waiting on you."

Terri walked out of the bedroom and went to the other side of the house. She picked up her phone and tried to call her husband, but it kept going to the voicemail. After three attempts, she called Patricia.

"Hey, Terri! I was just thinking about you! Where's Vas?"

"He's over to his grandmother's. Say could you come over ASAP? And bring your gun. I got problems."

"Say no more. On my way."

They hung up and Terri noticed that Victor had just walked in the room.

"I thought you said you had something in the oven. You lied."

Dread took over Terri's body. She couldn't answer.

"You're a sneaky bitch. So, you know, huh? You know I'm not Vincent, right?"

"Yeah. You can't be V. Victor?"

"Yep."

"What are you doing here?"

"I'm not going to hurt you…physically, that is. I was hoping you wouldn't find out. I was going to fuck you for old times' sake. Damn, I hate that didn't happen. But that's okay, I guess. You're going to get fucked anyway. Left you a little present on the bed."

"Victor?"

"Yeah, Terri, what's up?"

"Get the hell out of my house. **Now**, motherfucker!"

She was terrified, but she stood her ground. She didn't think to and now didn't have time to get her gun, but she was confident that Pat was on her way.

"Sure, gladly. It was good to see you again, even if you're not glad to see me. I'm leaving."

"That's probably a good idea. Pat's on her way over and if I tell her to shoot your ass, she'll do it and ask questions later. Do you understand?"

"I do. Enjoy your present…bitch!"

With that, Victor walked out the front door and left the door open, jumped into his vehicle and sped off. Terri slammed the door shut and then tried time and time again to reach V, but there was never an answer. Just a busy signal. This alarmed her and pissed her off at the same time. Pat pulled up, got out and rang the doorbell. Terri opened the door and hugged Pat, sobbing.

"What's wrong, Terri?"

"Victor was just here" she said between her sobs.

"Victor? How? Are you okay? Did he touch you?"

"No…well, yes but he didn't hurt me."

"Victor, huh? Where's V?"

"I don't really know. I've been trying to reach him but it either keeps going to voice mail or it's busy. Damn, Victor was in my damn house!"

"Well did he say what he wanted? I thought he was out of the states."

"He may have been, but he's not now."

"How do you know it was Victor?"

"V and I have a safe phrase and Victor didn't answer correctly. He really didn't say what he wanted…well, except for to fuck me but he did say he left me a present in the bedroom, but I'm afraid to go in there to get it. Could you…?"

Pat drew her gun.

"Yeah, girl. Stay behind me."

"Pat?"

"Yeah, Terri."

"Victor almost had sex with me! Do you know what that would have meant?" She shuddered at the thought.

"I know, girl. I'm here now. No worries."

CHAPTER 14

TWO STEPS AHEAD

V called Moms.
"Hello?"
"Hey, Moms! How you doing?"
"I'm fine, baby. How are you?"
"I'm good. Have you heard from Terri? I've been trying to reach her all day, but it keeps going to voicemail. Have you heard anything or seen her?"
"Earlier. She brought Vas to me. That little booger is a handful! He's worse than you and your brother!"
"Is that a bad thing?"
"No, I'm just saying. He's well behaved, but he's as busy as a fly trapped in a spider web! He's no problem at all."
"That's good. Tell him his Daddy said 'hi', but wait until I get off the phone. I'm getting ready to have an important meeting and I know him. He'll want to get on the phone and keep me there and I don't have that kind of time today. So, Moms…are you okay?"
"Yeah, boy, I told you I was fine."
"Yeah, well I'm concerned."
"Vinny, you're talking like something is wrong. Is something wrong?"
"Naw, Moms, everything is fine. I'm just checking up on you, that's it. No unwanted visitors?"
"No. Now, let me get back to this child of yours before he tears up something."
"I thought you just said he wasn't a problem to you!"
"He's not, Vinny but I do need to check on him."

"Okay, Moms. I'll talk to you later. Call me if you hear from Terri, okay or for anything for that matter."

"Alright, baby. Bye."

"Bye, Moms."

After V and Moms hung up, Vas came running up to Moms with something in his hands.

"Here, Mammaw!"

"Boy, what is that? Where did you get this from?"

"The mailman gave it to me and told me to give it to you."

"It's nicely wrapped. There's no return address on it. I wonder who could have sent...oh. I bet this is from Tony. That man! Let's see what's inside."

Moms unwrapped the package and opened the box that it covered. Inside, she would find a CD cover with a DVD enclosed. On the outside of the cover it read 'What you didn't know'. She took the DVD over to the player and put it in. She held Vas around his body between her legs while she sat down to view the tape. Moms was in unbelief. She rewound the DVD to make sure she didn't miss something. What she saw made Moms loosen her grip on her grandson and tighten her grip over her heart. Moms crumpled to the floor in a heap.

"Mammaw! Mammaw! Mammaw, get up!" Vas called out.

No answer; no response. Vas sat on the floor and put Moms head in his lap and then picked up her cell phone.

* * *

"Okay, I appreciate you all taking time from your busy schedules to be here but I will be honest with you all. I'm facing a serious situation."

V had his most trusted friends and associates to meet with him at the firm his brother once owned. He would always have access to the building when needed and it was a lot more discreet than his own place of business. Besides, he didn't want his employees to know about any dealings other than the security services business. Chase Morton, his trusted accountant; Belinda Jett, an associate of the firm who had proven her worth with V when he sold the company from under his brother's nose; and Marco and Alphonso, who had become his trusted allies who got things done when they needed to get done.

"What's the situation, V?" Chase asked.

"Victor Taylor is back in town."

Everyone got silent.

"How do you know? Have you seen him?" Belinda asked.

"Nope. Haven't seen him, but he's already tipped his hand. It appears he visited an old friend in prison. The Warden thought it was me and now that old friend is dead. I can see Victor doing something like that."

"Yeah, me too" said Alphonso. "He's probably pissed at me and Marco."

"I guarantee you that Victor is pissed at a lot of people, so watch your backs."

"So why are we here, I mean, specifically?" Chase asked.

"We are here to plan to work and work out a plan. A plan that protects us; physically as well as financially. If we want to win a game with that snake of a brother of mine, we have to keep two steps ahead of him."

"Well, I'll tell you, Mr. Taylor. I don't want to die. I don't want to lose my position, either. When Chase left the firm, it was I who was chosen by the board to run it. They wanted the best and I proved to them who that would be. I know I hadn't been there long, but I outperformed everyone except Chase."

"Yes, Ms. Jett, you have proven yourself over and over again. I thank you for what you did for me, but I'm asking for your help once more."

"Mr. Taylor, you've been nothing but nice to me, ever since I came here. Okay, you're not Victor Taylor, but that doesn't change the fact that if it weren't for you, I wouldn't be where I am. I'm here for you."

"Thanks, Belinda. How about the rest of you? Are you here for me, as well?"

Everyone in attendance was on board without hesitation. It mattered not what the plan was or what was required. They were ready to put in the work for a friend and they all considered Vincent Taylor their friend.

"Okay, V" Marco said, "what do we have to do?"

They all leaned in as V laid out the plan.

CHAPTER 15

PLAYA

"Damn, girl! You feel so good!"
Vance was on top of and inside of Cassie, sexing her down.

"You feel good, too Victor."

"Yeah, about that." Vance rolled over in the bed, off of her.

"What's wrong?" she asked.

"I have to tell you something. You might get mad."

"What is it, baby?" she said, stroking his chest.

"I'm not Victor" Vance lied, but telling the truth, as well.

"**What?!**"

"I'm not Victor. I'm V."

This was all a part of Victor's plan.

"V? You mean to tell me that you're Vincent? I thought you were gone out of the states! You played me! You bastard!"

"Now, don't be like that, Cassie. I found out about you and Victor but I knew he wouldn't be good for you. I knew you weren't true to me, but I couldn't get you out of my mind. I just couldn't let you go. That's why I'm back, baby."

Cassie just stared at Vance.

"Let me see your hand."

Vance showed her his right hand.

"No, I mean your other hand. Your *'married'* hand."

Vance then showed his left hand.

"Huh. No ring lines. I didn't even think to look earlier. Shit, the only thing different about you is how cut you are in the midsection. Your lovemaking techniques are a little different, I must admit. It's good…damn good, but definitely different. I just thought you had been working out since you left…well, obviously you have, but…you're not Victor, huh?"

"No. It's the truth."

"And you still want to be with me? After what I did to you?"

"Yes. Passing years can help a person heal, you know."

"Well…hey, there V. You want to finish what you started? I like the attention you're giving me. And baby?"

"Yeah."

"Can I apologize to you for that Victor escapade? He made promises and I ain't gonna lie; he hooked me up financially."

"Well, now I can lace you. It took a minute, but I got something solid now. And sure, you can apologize, but as you can tell, I've already accepted your apology."

Cassie raised the sheet and looked between Vance's legs.

"Yeah, I can see that. Sorry if I hurt you."

"No problem. Just don't let it happen again. I may not be so forgiving next time. Now roll over and get on your knees. Let me finish this."

"Yes sir, Mr. Taylor."

* * *

V pulled up to Moms house and was greeted by an ambulance in front of her house. He ran over to the EMT just as he and another attendant loaded his mom in the back of the vehicle.

"What happened!?" V asked.

"It appears she had a heart attack. You are…?"

"I'm her son. Vincent Taylor. Did you find a little boy in there?"

"Yeah, he's in the front seat. Your son?"

"Yeah."

"Smart little boy. He called 911. He couldn't give an address but it's good that the receptionist knew who Moms was. We got here as soon as we could."

"Yeah, the receptionist called me, too. Is she going to be okay? Do you know what happened?"

"It's pretty bad. I'd say it was a heart attack. All I can say is she's still alive for now."

"Can I take my son with me?"

"Sure. Young man" the EMT said to Vasyl, while walking to the passenger side, "do you know this man?"

"Daddy!" Vas said as he reached for V. V grabbed his son and held him close.

"Hey, Vas. Are you okay?"

"Yeah, Daddy. What's wrong with Mammaw?"

"She's gonna be okay. Do you know what happened, Vas?"

"All I know is she got this box in the mail and she watched this short movie. When she watched it, she fell on the floor."

"Okay. Let's go inside and get that movie, okay?"

"Okay, Daddy. Then we go home, right? I'm tired."

"Alright. I'll drop you off with Mama and I have to go to the hospital to be with your Mammaw."

V went in Moms' house with Vas, grabbed the DVD without looking at it, locked up the house and headed down the road with son in tow.

CHAPTER 16

CAN'T I HAVE BOTH?

V pulled up to his home and pulled in the circular driveway. Much the way Victor did it earlier. He honked his horn...much like Victor did earlier. He got out and got his son out of the back seat. By the time he did, the door opened.

"Where the hell you been? I've tried to call you all day!" Terri interrogated.

"I tried to call you, too. I've been at work all day. Had a big meeting."

"Yeah, well I didn't get any calls from you. I just bet you did have a big meeting."

"What do you mean by that? I gotta go."

"Where the fuck you going now!?"

"Moms had a heart attack."

"A heart attack!? What happened!?"

"I don't know. What's up, Terri? Why the attitude?"

"You should already know. Bastard."

Pat was standing behind Terri, peering over her shoulder, looking at V with disgust.

"Bastard? What? Look, I have to go. Whatever it is that's bugging you, we'll have to talk about it later. Okay?" V said.

"Yeah...if I'm still here."

"Why would you not be here?"

Pat spoke up.

"Boy, go see about your mother. You guys will talk when you talk."

"Pat, I love you, but mind your business, okay? I'll call you later, Terri. Unless you want to come to the hospital with me now."

"If I do come to the hospital, I'll come with Pat."

"Alright. I gotta go."

V sped off down the highway while Pat and Terri watched him drive down the road.

He thought, *what's bugging her?*

"Girl, you should have put **his** ass out instead of moving out yourself," Pat said.

"Pat, this is the house he built for himself. I'm not staying here. Every time I stay in one of these homes these brothers build, I wound up getting shitted on. Come on, help me finish packing."

Terri took Vas inside and went back to the bedroom with Pat.

* * *

Victor and Vance were in their hotel room watching TV. Victor lit up a cigar and grabbed him some Apple Crown on the rocks and got posted up for a super chill moment.

"What? Are you celebrating or something?" Vance asked.

"Not a complete celebration. Just a mini-celebration. I'm satisfied." Victor smiled, quite pleased with himself.

"Oh. So, what do we have planned for tomorrow?"

"Nothing. We lay low and chill for a day or two…let the pot simmer for a minute. Why? You got plans?"

"Not really. Just thought I'd get out and get my head right."

"Your head better already be right! Where you plan on going?"

"Nowhere in particular," Vance lied. "So, did you make that visit to finalize our transactions?"

"No, sorry. I've been busy with my own shit. Had to hit a couple of spots."

"Damn, Victor! I thought we were going to finish this and get the fuck out of here! The more you prolong, the longer we have to stay!"

"Okay, man, I'll handle that shit tomorrow or Friday."

"Well, I guess it's okay not to move too fast. We're okay."

"Wait a damn minute! You're going to see Cassie again, aren't you? Are you falling for that chick?"

"Naw, man!" Vance lied again.

Vance turned his attention back to the TV.

"But…what if I was?" he asked, without even turning away from the set.

"She'll fuck around on you. I know. But, hell, I don't care. Just don't you fuck up. I swear if you do…"

"P'shue! You know what? I'm not afraid of you. You may know me, but you don't know who I know or all that I know. Get my drift, punk!"

"Watch your mouth, boy. You don't know who I know either. The best damn thing you can do is keep your mouth shut, your eyes open and your feet to the ground. We're going to get your money, don't worry."

"Good. That's what I want."

Vance wanted the money, but now, he wanted Cassie, too. If he had his way, he would find a way to have them both when all was said and done.

CHAPTER 17

ON RECORD

When V reached the hospital, and headed to the room that Moms had been admitted to, he saw Sabino in the hallway talking on his cell phone.

"Yeah. Thanks for the info. Damn, man, you're on top of this, huh? You are! Okay, I'll see you then. Alright. No, I won't tell anyone. Bye."

He turned his attention toward Vincent.

"Hey, V. She's resting now. Do you know what happened?" Sabino asked.

"Not yet, but I wouldn't be surprised if Vic had something to do with this. I wish he'd turn up. I'd kick his ass right about now."

"Now don't do anything drastic. First of all, you need proof. Second of all, let him trip over his own shit. I got some important info I think you could use, but I'll tell you later. Go in and see your mama."

V entered the room to find Moms hooked up to all kinds of machines and monitors. The walls were sterile white and the room was cool. He walked over to her bedside. She seemed to be resting peaceably, so he didn't say anything to her. He just reached and grabbed her hand and said a prayer. *Don't ignore me, God. Not this time*, he thought. He stayed for a few minutes but he knew there was nothing he could do now but wait. He walked back out in the hallway. Sabino was still there.

"What you got for me?" V asked.

"A name. Professor Timothy Carr. Remember that and tell it to your people. That's it for now, but my sources say he's going to show up in your life real soon."

"Okay. I trust you. I've got to catch up with Terri. She's pissed off at me and I don't know why. I haven't done anything…wait. She must have found out about me leaving Moms the other day."

"Oh, that's why she called me to help her. You left."

"Moms called you? Damn. You two better slow down. I swear Sabino...Dad...if you hurt her I'm gonna hurt you. Understand?"

"I'm not gonna hurt her, son. But do us both a favor, okay?"

"What's that?"

"Stop threatening me. I might get upset. I would hate to lose one of my sons over some bullshit. Capisce?

"Oh, so, now you're threatening me? Remember, you're not really Sabino, so kiss my ass...Dad. Let me know if she wakes up." V said as he walked away from his father.

* * *

"Are you sure, Pat?" asked Jr.

"I saw the tape! It was V! It couldn't be Victor because he was with Terri. Terri confirmed that those were the clothes he had on when he left home. He said he was helping Moms...at least that's what his alibi was. The sad part is, it wasn't just one occasion. V was recorded twice! I'm just as upset as Terri is...well, maybe not as much as she is, but I'm pretty pissed off, too!"

"Damn. I need to call V and see what's up. That just doesn't sound like my boy. He loves Terri. Hell, he adores her. This just doesn't sound like the V I know."

"Yeah, well he should have thought about that before he decided to fuck around on his woman! You know what else is just as bad? He was with Cassie! Cassie said his damn name!"

"Not Cassie! His old girlfriend? Damn. Okay, let me get back at you and try to reach V. Love you, babe. Oh, and babe, you don't have to worry about me doing that to you. This I can and will prove. I'll holla at you later."

"Okay, baby. Let me know what you find out."

"Will do."

* * *

Sabino went into Moms room and sat in the chair that was not too far from her bed. He wasn't leaving. He sat there until he nodded off to sleep.

CHAPTER 18

MAJOR ROLES

V was in shock. When he reached his house, and parked in the garage, he went inside to find a DVD on his bed. He called out for Vas and Terri, but didn't get answer. He went to the bedroom with one DVD in his hand, only to see there was another one sitting on his bed, waiting for him to watch. He put the one that was on the bed in first only to be faced with a nightmare of a situation. Two clips on the same disc. One clip showed him in the T-shirt and jeans he had on the day he was supposed to help Moms and another showed him in the clothes he had on during his meeting. Both times showed him sexing Cassie. He knew it wasn't himself in the video, but it still didn't look good. His guess was it was Victor. The times on the video matched the times he was away, so unless he could prove otherwise, he looked guilty. This was just another situation in which he was accused of something he knew he didn't do. It was a feeling he had before, but he did not like. He started to call Terri, but he collected himself to look at the other DVD to see if it could have had anything to do with Moms condition. There again was a nightmare to behold. It showed the last time the brothers were together with Sabino. He relived the whole event, all the way to when Sabino pulled off his mask, revealing his true identity! Moms now knew. Even if Sabino, or Thomas Taylor, had left town, it wouldn't matter.

"Oh, Moms" he said with pain and sorrow in his heart and voice. He didn't mean to keep this information away from Moms, but he didn't want to hurt her. He winded up hurting her anyway. Not on purpose, but now the truth was out. V felt betrayed and all alone...again. Now's the time to call Terri.

"Hello" Terri answered coldly.

"Terri! Where are you, babe?"

"Somewhere."

"Are you over to Pat's? I'm coming to get you."

"No, I am not over to Pat's. I'm somewhere. And you're not coming to get me."

"Terri, baby, that's not…"

"What? That's not you on that video? Bullshit, V! When you came home from helping Moms at that catering affair, the clothes I washed the next day were the same clothes you had on that day. And then today? Same clothes. No answer of a cell phone. No true alibi. You know what? I don't want to talk to you anymore right now…"

"Terri! I know you don't, but that's not me on that tape! You know that's probably Victor, don't you? You know he's in town, right? Have you seen him?"

"Yeah, I saw him. He was over here the same time you were sexing Cassie!"

"Come on, baby, you know in your heart that I could never do that to you! Let me…"

Click! Terri hung up in V's face. V sat there, staring at his phone.

"Okay, Vic. I can see what you're doing. You want revenge? You wanna play hardball? Get ready, son, 'cause you're gonna be dropped to the minors! It's time you played against a professional! I'm coming to get you, rookie!"

* * *

"Yeah, I'm playing a major role. (pause) No, no, I shouldn't be in any danger. (pause) Don't worry about me. I trust Mr. Taylor. (pause) I'm thinking by the end of the week. (pause) Okay, I will. (pause) Are you going to come see me at Christmas? (pause) Well, I hope so. I miss you. (pause) I love you, too. Bye, love."

Belinda Jett loved to talk on the phone, but she knew she couldn't say too much. She tried to keep her boyfriend abreast as to things happening in her life. This time, though, she had to be vague. V counted on her too much and she certainly wouldn't be the one that messed everything up for everybody else. Her phone rang.

"Hello? Mr. Taylor?!"

"Hi, Belinda. Sorry for calling so late. Were you sleeping?"

"No sir, I'm up. Getting ready to turn in, though. What's up?"

"You are. Ha ha, just joking. Okay, prepare those special papers… you know the ones, and remember this name: Professor Timothy Carr. Got it?"

"Yes, sir I got it."

"Good. Well, that's all I wanted. Good night."

"Good night, sir."

Belinda hung up her phone and prepared for bed.

"Oh, shit…I mean, shoot, it's on now!"

CHAPTER 19

LEGALITIES

Chase Morton and Belinda Jett had just finished up gathering up the correct papers needed for V's plan to go off without a hitch. He shook her hand and walked out of her office. He stopped by Lisa, his fiancé's desk and gave her a kiss before getting on the elevator. Belinda ran the firm, but she would ask Chase for assistance when needed. He never was on a schedule, so he was glad to oblige when called upon. She put the papers in their own separate folders and then played the waiting game. She didn't have to wait long.

"Ms. Jett?" Lisa spoke over the intercom.

"Yes, Lisa."

"There is a Mr. Carr here to see you. Are you aware of this meeting?"

Even Lisa was instructed to play dumb.

"I am. Send him in."

Belinda took a deep breath but remained seated. She didn't want to get dizzy dealing with this individual, especially since she didn't know who he was or what he wanted. All she knew was that this was the name that V gave her. The door opened.

"Ms. Jett? My name is Timothy Carr. Professor Timothy Carr. I know you're probably busy but were you informed of my arrival?"

"No sir, Mr. Carr. I was made aware that someone of importance would be arriving, so I assume it is you, sir. Come in, have a seat. How can I be of assistance to you?"

"I know this might look strange and it may sound even stranger but your firm was at the top of my list and I need some legal services rendered."

"What type of services?" she asked.

"Well, it's sort of delicate. I'm sort of here on a dual basis. I need help, but I'll discuss that in a minute. I know this firm was purchased by a group of gentlemen a few years back, but I also represent a group of men who would like to purchase it, as well. If I'm not mistaken, this firm's last transactional endeavor, netted the seller $65 million. Am I correct?"

"Yes sir, it isn't hidden information. It's been publicized."

"Okay. Well, the gentlemen I represent would like to make an offer for the firm and we don't know who to reach. Would you be privy to that information?"

"Yes, I would. Please, go on."

"Oh, okay. Well, their offer is for $265 million. I told them that I thought it was a bit much, but they've stuck to their guns. I don't know what they see in this place, but they want to make this dream of theirs a reality."

"I see. So why you, Mr. Carr?"

"What?"

"Why are they using you to execute their transactions? They couldn't come here themselves?"

"Oh!" Victor laughed. "I have been very successful in my past dealings with them. You know, golf courses, travel clubs, real estate, etc. I usually walk in without a deal and walk out with one. I'm sort of the 'Tronald Dump' of deals, you see."

"Don't you mean, Donald…never mind. I see. Well, Mr. Carr…I'm sorry; Professor Carr…"

"Mr. Carr is fine. Professor Carr is my name when I'm teaching at the college."

"Oh? What college, sir?"

"The Virginia Tech Carilion School of Medicine. Didn't know that existed, did you?"

"No sir, I wasn't aware. How long have they been established?"

"Since 2010"

"Oh, okay. Well, Mr. Carr, I know your intentions and I will pass this information to the proper people."

"Thank you. But that was only one item I had to discuss with you. One of my benefactors is having trouble accessing a particular bank account. It appears there are some legalities holding up a process. Do you think you can help me…uh, him?"

"If you said 'legalities', then I believe there may be something we could do."

"Great! Now listen closely. We don't need any mistakes with this one."

Belinda took out her notepad and wrote what Victor, alias Professor Timothy Carr told her. When he finished, they shook hands and he left. Belinda got on the intercom.

"Lisa, find me all you can about a Virginia Tech Carilion Medicine. And get me Mr. Taylor on the line."

CHAPTER 20

ACTION JACKSON

Vance had a plan. Victor had a plan. Now, Vincent had a plan and the main part of his plan was finding Terri. He was at the hospital at the moment, questioning the attending nurse.

"So, there's been no change?"

"No sir. She's still out."

"Damn. Do you have any idea how long she will be this way?"

"It's hard to tell. We hooked her up to the EKG machine and her heart took a pretty hard beating. She's strong, though, right?"

"Yeah, Moms is the strongest woman I know, but when it comes to health and a heart attack, hell who knows?"

"Yes. Well, we're monitoring her and we are doing all we can to get her back up and running. Trust us, Mr. Taylor, we're taking as good a care for your mother as we would anyone."

"Thanks. Don't spare any expense, okay? Look, I have to run. Do you think it will be okay leaving her now?"

"Oh, yes sir, we have your number, right?"

V nodded.

"We'll just call you if she wakes up, okay?"

"Please do. Thanks for everything."

V walked out the hospital and pulled out his cell.

"Hey, Marco. Did our pigeon show up at the firm?"

"Yeah. Me and Alphonso were dressed as janitors and he didn't even pay us no never mind."

"Cool. Ya'll tagging him now?"

"Yep. We'll know where he lives by the end of today. I'll call you when we find out."

"Very cool! Oh, and Marco? Could you try to locate Terri? It's been a couple of days and she is super pissed at me. She left me, you know."

"Aw, sorry about that, V. We didn't know. We'll put some feelers out for her. We'll find her."

"Thanks man. Please call me as soon as you do. Oh, and pick up my laundry for me."

"Your laundry? Okay. Gotcha. Will do."

They hung up and V dialed another number.

"Hello, Belinda."

"Hello, Mr. Taylor. I tried to reach you."

"Sorry, I must have missed your call. I understand he came. Professor Carr, that is. You know that was Victor, don't you?"

"I figured. His makeup was on pretty good; gray eyes and all."

"Gray? Never mind, it doesn't matter. So, did he talk?"

"Boy, did he! He's trying to get your money."

"Figures. That's not a problem. You gave him the numbers he asked for, didn't you?"

"Yes, sir. Was I not supposed to?"

"Oh, yes I needed you to. He doesn't realize how much I need him to try to get my money, anyway."

"Huh?"

"Don't worry about it. I'll fill you in when the time is right."

"Okay. Is that all you need, sir? I have an important meeting with the owners of the firm in about ten minutes and I need to prepare myself. This is part of your plan, sir."

"Okay, I won't hold you. Take care of business and I'll holla back later."

"Alright, sir. Be careful."

"You, too, Ms. Jett."

V hung up and made one more call. He just realized he was missing an important component to this whole ordeal. He would rectify that immediately.

"Hello? May I speak to Special Agent Martin? Jr. Martin. Yes, I'll wait. (pause) Yes, hello? Tell him it's Vincent Taylor. I missed his call the other day and I'm returning it. Thank you. (pause) Hey, Jr.! Yeah, man I missed it and for some reason, I couldn't reach you on your cell. Anyway, when can you come home? I need you, dude."

CHAPTER 21

Dirty Laundry

Vance and Victor were having a conversation on the phone.
"So, she left his ass, huh? Cool! How many days ago?"
"I'm not sure, but I know it's been a couple," Vance said.
"Hell, I've got so many things going on, I'm out of the loop! So, did you put a tail on her?"
"I've got people."
"Good. Where is she now? Or do you even know?"
"Yeah, I know. It'll cost you, though."
"What the fuck! You're hustling me?"
"Naw, my brother. I'm charging you. Are you paying?"
"How much?"
"Let's see…since you're family, how about $100 million? You know, chump change."
"You fucking bastard! Okay, deal. Do you really know where she is?"
"I really do. Do we really have a deal? Remember, your word better be your bond."
"I said, deal, boy. Where is she right now?"
"She's at Macy's."
"Hell, I'm right around the corner from there! I'm fixing to have me some fun!"
"Don't fuck up, Vic."
"Naw, don't you fuck up! She better be there."
"She is."
Victor hung up the phone and sped to Macy's. He went in and saw this woman from behind, with the shape of Terri, wearing black yoga pants with pink stripes down the side, a matching sports bra and pink

70

and gray Brooks Glycerin 14 running shoes. She had on a headband that covered her ears. He walked up to her, slowly. It was only when she turned around, was he sure.

"Hey, there. It's a bit cold to be walking around town dressed like that. Are you still mad at me?"

She turned around to face her inquisitor.

"Naw, I ain't mad at you. Mad at you for what? I don't even know you."

"Aw, Terri, don't be like that. I'm sorry for what I did. Let me make it up to you."

"What did you just call me?"

"Terri. Why?"

"Because at first, I was wondering how you knew my name, but then you almost got it right. It's not the first time happening."

"Huh?"

"The name is Kerri. And you are…?"

"Oh, you want to play games, huh? Okay, my name is, uh…Romeo."

"That's not your real name, is it?" she asked.

"Well, is Kerri your real name?"

"Yes, it is. Do I know you or something? I just got in this town yesterday and I don't know anyone."

"Stop playing, Terri."

Kerri just looked at Victor. She was through trying to explain who she was.

"Really? Your name really is Kerri and not Terri?"

"Yes, I already told you."

"Damn, you look just like…"

"Just like this girl you know, I bet. I've heard that a couple of times already. Sort of lets me know I'm on the right path."

"The right path to what?"

"Finding my twin sister. You know, the name you called me. Terri."

* * *

Cassie happened to be shopping at Macy's as well and saw when Victor stepped to who he thought was Terri. She couldn't hear the conversation and she kept her distance, but she witnessed the whole thing. She figured it to be Victor and not who she thought was Vincent…

she hoped, anyway. Just to be sure, she called who she thought was Vincent but was really Vance.

"Hey, Sugar!" Vance answered.

"Hey, Babes! How are you?"

"I'm fantastic, now! And you?"

"Well, I started to get a little confused until I called you."

"How so?"

"Well, I was over here in the lingerie section…you already know what for…and I saw what I thought was you stepping to Terri, but since I'm still looking at them and talking to you, I'm okay now."

"Good. I miss you. I can't wait to see you later."

"Me, too."

"Look, sorry about this, but I've got to go, but I'll see you tonight, okay?"

"Okay. Same place?"

"It's been lucky for us so far."

"Yeah, it has! See ya later. Bye."

Cassie decided to sneak out of the store without being seen, since she was relieved the man she saw was not her man. After she paid for her sheer items, she stepped outside the building and headed for her car. Seemingly out of nowhere, a black Hummer rolled up beside her and Marco and Alphonso jumped out, grabbed her and put her in the backseat with one of them. They took off down the road until they were out of sight.

"Hello? Yeah, we got your laundry. On our way to the cleaners," Marco said to V on the phone.

"Good. I'll shoot more info to Sabino once you guys get there."

"Gotcha."

No sooner than the Punishers with passenger in tow, were out of sight, Victor and Kerri were leaving the store together. They went to where he was parked and Kerri got in with Victor and they were on their way to God knows where. No sooner than those two left and were out of sight, Terri stepped outside of the store, bags in tow.

CHAPTER 22

222 Reasons

Vance paced up and down in the hotel room. No matter how many times he called Cassie, he didn't get an answer. He actually started to worry, but he wouldn't confide with Victor. Victor was watching a boxing match on the TV but he noticed how fidgety Vance was.

"Damn, dude, sit your ass down! What's the problem? Shit! You're making me nervous," Victor said to Vance.

"I can't reach Cassie. We were supposed to hook up."

"You're acting like a damn girl. Sit down."

Vance sat in the chair and looked at his phone.

"I wonder what happened. This ain't like her. I talked to her earlier."

"Okay. Maybe she's busy. You know Terri left V, so maybe she hooked up with him thinking it's you."

"Kiss my ass, Vic. She would know the difference."

"How do you know? Your people you had tailing Terri got it wrong; maybe she could too."

"What do you mean they got it wrong? You caught up with Terri, didn't you?"

"Naw…even better. I met Terri's twin, Kerri."

"Terri's twin!? Twin?! Did you know she had a twin?"

"Naw, she never mentioned it. That just lets me know that Terri ain't as innocent as she plays. But, man, this girl was her splitting image."

"Did she have on a blue pantsuit?"

"No. She wore some workout clothes. That booty was looking right, too!"

73

"Shit! My people were tailing Terri and she had on a blue pantsuit. Hell, it's too cold for someone to be walking around with just workout clothes. You just lucked up in running into this girl. I'll bet if you checked, a purchase was made by Terri. So, this girl you met was named Kerri and she said she was Terri's twin sister?"

"Yep. We hooked up. I should be mad at you for fucking that up. I really want to dick that girl. Terri, that is, but hey, Kerri will do."

"So, you dicked Kerri, instead?"

"Not after first meeting her, no. Won't be too long, though. I plan on it. Fine is fine and Kerri is just as fine as Terri, so hitting that ass ought to feel real good. She's a little rougher than Terri is. I like that. Come to think about it, this might prove to be advantageous in the end. I'm gonna use this info to my favor."

"How?" Vance asked.

"You just worry about your woman…I'll worry about my women. Hell, come to think about it, Cassie is still mine, too."

Vance jumped up from the seat he was in and headed towards Victor. Victor pulled out a Dan Wesson ECO 1911 9mm pistol from under his lap.

"Sit your ass back down, boy!" Vic said while pointing the gun at his brother. Vance slowly backed up and sat back in the chair.

"When did you get that?"

"Today."

"That cost you a pretty penny, I bet."

"Over $1400."

"I hope you don't plan on using that on anyone."

"If no one gives me a reason, I won't. If I feel threatened…well, I know how to use it."

*　*　*

"Why are you holding me here? You don't have any rights, you know. This is kidnapping. If you let me go now, I promise I want press charges."

Cassie was seated at a table while Marco and Alphonso stood in front of her, not talking.

"Look, if you don't let me go, I'm gonna scream!"

Alphonso stepped in front of the table.

"Scream if you want to and I will slap the shit out of you! Now shut the hell up, bitch!"

Cassie went silent, but she couldn't control the tears that were coming down her face. The door opened and a large figure came in.

"So, you're Ms. Cassandra, huh? Nice. Look, chick, we're not going to hurt you…that is, if you cooperate with us."

Sabino was laying it all out for Ms. Cassie.

"You see, we know all about your fooling around on Vinny with Victor and we know about you hooking back up with who you think is Vinny."

"I don't know what you're talking about," she said.

"Bitch, don't lie to me! Do you understand how much trouble you're in? No, I don't think so. Now there has always been one thing for sure about you: you don't love either one of those boys, but you sure as hell love the money. So, we are going to make you a proposition that neither one of them will make. You don't want someone dishing out money to you, do you? You want your own money, am I right?"

Cassie nodded.

"Okay, so this is what we need from you. That boy you're hanging out with has some information we can use. Now, you get that information for us, you live and we will make it worth your while. Hold on."

Sabino looked at his phone as he received a text.

"Damn! Really!? Okay. Just received a text from my boss. He said to offer you $222 million. You could live off of that by yourself, couldn't you, Sweetie?"

Cassie nodded again, wide-eyed and never taking them off of Sabino.

"Okay, now listen close. I'm going to lay it down and you're going to pick it up, Capisce?"

Cassie nodded once more and then had her head filled with the plan to infiltrate the enemy and bring back the info needed by even more enemies. When Sabino finished, he made sure she understood.

"Now, you do understand you can tell us no, right? However, if you do, you won't live to see tomorrow. Any questions?"

"Only one…why did you say I'm with who I *think* is V?"

"Oh…just making conversation, that's all."

CHAPTER 23

SICK CALL

Monday morning. The weekend was like a blur to V. He woke up without his family and it was killing him. His mother was in the hospital with no change in her condition. He hoped she was getting a well-needed rest. Victor was back in town, causing havoc. V felt so bad about everything and regretted not telling Moms about Sabino, not telling Terri about the other day with the classmate and not telling Victor the truth about the contract he signed. He shouldn't have been so naïve, but he should have known that one day, Victor would come back seeking restitution. He felt...no, he *knew* Vic would try to hurt him, but he never figured he'd try to hurt Moms.

"Damn, my son's birthday is next week!" he blurted out. "And right now, I can't even see him. Fucking Victor! Boy, I swear when I get my hands on you...no...I actually need you. So damn stupid, you don't even know it."

V got up and went to the bathroom. He looked in the mirror and before he saw his own face, he saw Victor's. He almost punched the mirror, but caught himself. He washed his face, brushed his teeth and then jumped in the shower. The water felt good against his skin. He hoped it would wash away his worries and stress, but when he got out, he was still facing the fact that Terri was not with him...and it hurt like hell! He went back into the bedroom and got dressed, but not in his typical suit and tie for work. He grabbed a pair of jeans, a t-shirt, his Timberland boots, his wool coat and his cell phone. He called his office.

"Hey, Karen? I won't be there today, so take messages for me. If it seems important, call me. Otherwise, I'm calling in sick."

"That's a first, Mr. Taylor. I never heard of a boss calling in sick to his own company."

"Well, I guess that's just my nature…a pioneer. Ha ha! I'm not sick, per se, but I won't be there today. I'm dealing. You understand, right? Tell everyone to work only half a day. I'll pay them for a full one. I'll try to be there tomorrow."

"Okay, Mr. Taylor. Whatever you're going through, I hope everything works out. By the way, how's your mom?"

"Same. Thanks for asking. I'll holla back and you have a good day, okay?"

"You too, sir."

V hung up and headed out the door…just not sure where to go.

"Terri, please give me the chance to fix this," he said to himself as he started his car. He drove down the road and prepared to try to call his wife when his phone rang.

"Jr? You're coming in when? Okay, I'll pick you up. I won't tell her."

* * *

"What happened, Baby? I was so worried. Where were you?"

Vance and Cassie were discussing the weekend. It had been two days and Vance hadn't heard from her until now. They were at their normal meeting spot: Vance's special hotel room away from he and Victor's hotel room. This time, however, there was no recording going on.

"I had to go check on an Uncle out of town. I thought I'd be back sooner than now, but where he stays there's no phone or satellite service. The whole town is a dead spot," Cassie lied.

"You don't understand! I thought something happened to you and I was worried as hell!"

"Aw, boo, you were worried about me?"

"Well…yeah!"

"How sweet. Well, as you can see, I'm fine. But I've been thinking about something."

"What's that?"

"Well…you say that you couldn't get me off of your mind and you still wanted to be with me, even after you found out about me and Victor. If that's true, why did you wait four whole years to get back to me? What are you really into? I mean, if we're going to move forward, shouldn't we practice being honest and truthful to each other?"

Vance looked at Cassie and in his mind, he knew he wanted to be with her for a long time. Wasn't sure about marriage, but he wasn't ruling it out, either. She was his Cinderella and he wanted to be her Prince Charming. He didn't want Victor mad at him, but this plan was his, not Vic's and if he wanted to change it, he would.

"Yeah, it looks sort of funky, doesn't it? I probably shouldn't do this, but for some reason, I trust you. I've come into some money, or couldn't you already tell?"

"I could tell. You've never had the money to stay in a place like this. I'd figure you would stay with Moms. By the way, I heard she had a heart attack. How is she?"

Vance hadn't heard, so he didn't know. His people he had keeping up with other items, wasn't keeping up with Moms, since she played no part in his equations. Although the issue at hand was honesty and truthfulness, he had to lie.

"I hadn't heard anything lately, so she must be still resting."

"Okay, that's good. Maybe we can go visit her together."

"Yeah, maybe."

"Cool. So, you were saying something about coming into some money?"

"Oh, yeah. Anyway, I've come into some, but I found out that more was due me. I knew you were high-maintenance, and I had to go and make mine so you could have the finer things. I've been away, true, but I've never stop thinking about you. I only want the best for you."

"Do you?"

"I really do."

"Come here, Sugar," Cassie said.

Vance stood up and approached Cassie. She kissed him softly and embraced him deeply. She put her head on his chest and just held him.

"Do you want me to make love to you?" Vance asked.

"No. Just let me hold you for a moment."

She started to regret what she had to do, and she hated what she was already doing, but she really didn't have a choice. She had to totally win him over so that he would divulge. As much as she didn't want to, the choice between not living and living with over $200 million dollars, was not a hard one…even if it hurt someone she cared about.

CHAPTER 24

WASTED ENERGY

Terri and Pat decided to eat lunch at McAlister's.

"Girl, I'm not one to start any shit in someone else's life, but do you know what you are going to do…other than just move out?" Pat asked.

"Pat, I don't know what to do. Vas is asking where his father is and why can't we go home and I don't really have any answers for him. I don't know. In all fairness, I probably should hear V's side. He's never done anything like this…at least, as far as I know. He's so attentive and loving. This shit is hard to take."

"And you're sure it's not Victor on those videos."

"Yeah, pretty sure. I mean, it adds up, or it don't add up, whichever. The time on that video was the same time V should have been with Moms, but clearly, he wasn't. I can't ask Moms, 'cause she's out. It's only V's word against that video. You know what makes it worse? It was a couple of times! The second time, I tried to call him all damn day and it just kept going to his voicemail. What am I supposed to do, Pat? Just be a stupid little girl?"

"Terri, I'll tell you something. My FBI instincts are tingling and they're telling me that **that** is not V on that video. Yeah, maybe you should…hey, isn't that those two bruisers I met at V's birthday party years ago?"

Pat motioned to the counter, where Marco and Alphonso was ordering cokes for themselves. Terri had to look over her shoulder, since her back was to the door.

"Yeah, that's Marco and Alphonso."

"Well, they're coming this way. Do I need to get my gun ready?"

"Naw, girl…hell, I don't know…you might!"

They laughed. The boys walked up to the table.

"Hello, ladies. May we join you for a minute?" Alphonso asked.

"We were just leaving," Pat responded.

"Oh, that's okay, this won't take but a minute," said Marco.

Terri offered them seats.

"Please. Have a seat, gentlemen."

"Thank you, Terri. Terri, V is a mess. He wouldn't tell us what was going on, but he did say that whatever this is that has you all twisted, he's innocent about it! Why won't you talk to him; hear his side of the story?" Marco asked.

"I might. I'm just so damn mad right now!"

"Let me ask you something. What if you're wrong in your thinking? That would be a lot of wasted negative energy towards something that could have been cleared up days ago. Don't youse agree?" Alphonso interjected. "Sorry…don't **you** agree? I'm trying to speak better."

Pat started to answer, but Terri stopped her.

"No, Pat, I got this. You know what fellas, I **do** agree with you. I would have wasted all this time dealing with my emotions for nothing! You know what, you're pretty smart…to be a…what are you two, anyway?"

"Just two guys who care. But I will tell you this so you won't get spooked; we have a tail on you and we knew you were here. We know where you're staying, but…we won't tell V; not yet, anyway. When you are ready to talk to him, call him. But just like we're not telling him where you are, please don't tell him we already knew. You think Victor's a beast? Shiiit! V's the beast…especially when it comes to those he cares about and he will make sure we get fucked up! Excuse my French," Marco spoke.

"I understand. I won't tell him anything he doesn't need to know. Let me think some more about what to do. I know you have to report back to him so tell him I went underground or some shit like that. I'll call him; soon."

"Okay. Ms. Martin, it was good to see you again. We'll leave you ladies to your lunch. Have a nice day," said Alphonso.

"You sirs do the same," Pat replied.

With that, the two men got up and walked out of the restaurant.

"Go figure," Pat said.

"What's that?"

"That you would get a psychological lecture from a bruiser like that."

"Yeah, he made sense. They both did. It's obvious they care about V."

"We all do, girl. The question now is, is he worth it?"

Terri looked out the window at the snow that had already fallen and made the town a Winter Wonderland.

"Deep down in my heart, Pat… I know he is."

* * *

Sabino was busy trying to make sure that small orders were filled at Moms catering business. He had the keys to her building, so all he had to do now, was find the orders and make sure they were filled. He could cook a little, but he knew he couldn't do justice to what Moms was putting out, so he shut down Elaine's for now and brought his chefs from that restaurant over to Moms to take care of business. He knew of one order in particular that would have been extremely important to Moms and it was the annual Christmas Gala that was coming up this very weekend. It was put on by Vincent, starting two years ago and it has been such a success, that they just couldn't put it off this year…even if Moms was on her back. There was one problem, however. It seems as if **everyone** that had been involved with it before, had forgotten that it was coming up. **Everyone!** V; Terri; Pat; and Jr. Everyone was so preoccupied with their lives; this function completely slipped their minds. Sabino knew he had to fix that situation. He pulled out his phone and dialed.

"Hello, V? Did you forget about your annual thing?"

"What annual thing?" V asked.

"Your Gala."

"Oh, shit! That's this coming weekend, isn't it?! Okay. I know what to do. Thanks, Dad."

"You're welcome, son. Did you find Ter…?"

V hung up before Sabino could ask. Sabino smiled, knowing he was doing right by Moms and he contacted the right person to make this all pop off.

CHAPTER 25

BOY SCOUT

"So, what's this I hear about you and Cassie fucking again?" V had picked Jr. up from the airport and Jr. lit into him as soon as they headed down the road. "It's not true, dude. I ain't fucked no one but Terri since I've been out of prison. I mean, I ain't **slept** with no one but Terri. We make love."

"Whatever. Pat tells me there's video. How are you getting past that?"

"Man, you know me! And Victor's back in town."

"What!? When did he get back in town? Pat didn't tell me that. I thought he signed a contract to stay away forever?"

"Pat didn't tell you, huh? He did sign a contract, but it wasn't for forever."

"No?"

"Naw. Victor got so careless at the end of that ordeal that he didn't even read the damn contract. First of all, since we agreed that whoever was determined to be 'Vincent'…me…that person would have to be the one who left, right?"

"Right."

"Well, he didn't even realize that he even signed that agreement, but once he did, he honored it. Anyway, what he didn't do, was look further into the contract. It clearly stated that he could return to the states after 365 days. Victor was so into his feelings, he got sloppy. I expected him to be back three years ago! I've never seen him so careless."

"You're shitting me, aren't you?"

"Man, I wouldn't shit you…you're my favorite turd!"

V laughed, but stopped quickly. He hadn't had anything to laugh about lately and it felt uncomfortable.

"Very funny. So, you're telling me that that is not you in the video, but Victor?"

"It has to be, because it sure as hell ain't me!"

"Okay, man. I believe you. But now you have to prove it, you know that, right?"

"Yeah, I know. That's what I'm working on now. But you want to know something else? Victor has come back to hurt and for that he has to pay."

"Really? He wants revenge, huh?"

"Hell, yeah. You know Moms had a heart attack, right?" V asked.

"I heard. Is she going to be okay?"

"I sure hope so. Victor's behind that, too. I know everyone has their day to die, right? I'm just not ready for it to be Moms' time."

"I know, right?"

There was an awkward silence between the best friends.

"So…wait a minute. You expected Victor to come back sooner than now? You have a reason, don't you?"

"Damn, Jr., how in the hell did you deduce that?"

"FB…"

"I. Yeah, I know. You're good, man, I'll give you that, and you're right, too. I need Victor for a particular reason, but he won't raise his head. I'm not going to just swoop him up. He's still the attorney, and I don't need any legal bullshit on me right now. Besides, it might spook him and I'll still be waiting on what I need. But now that you're back, I need you to play ghost, but investigate. Hell, now I'm glad I didn't tell Pat you were coming in. You're not coming in. I need you to tail the tail. My people are real close to disclosing his location, but they can't do it like you. I still don't know how he gave them the slip when he left the firm last week. So, I need you to see what you can do. Cool?"

"Yeah, I'm cool with that. You do realize I'm on another tail, don't you? I might get a phone call and if I do, I'll have to drop you. How do you know you're not being watched right now?"

"I don't, but I know how to get you in town without anyone knowing. You know what I'm talking about, right?"

"Our plan from two years ago? Damn, V it's too damn cold for that!"

"That's what friends are for, right? I'll take your stuff over to my house…seeing as there's no one there but me. You keep your coat. You know how to make a fire, don't you?"

"Yes. Yes, I do."

"Good, because it's fixing to get real hot...or cold, in your case."

* * *

"Say, Vic, you do know your mother had a heart attack, right?" Vance asked.

"I heard."

"You heard!? You haven't gone to see her!?"

"Not yet. Might bump into V and I don't want that...not just yet, anyway."

"Damn, man, you're heartless! If that was my mother, I'd…"

"Now, you're about to say the dumbest shit ever. That is your mother, jack-ass! Go see her, if that's what you want to do."

"What I meant to say is, if that was my **mama**…the woman who raised me, I would be up there in a snap. I know she is my mother, but I have no emotional ties with that woman. Hell, she gave me away! She didn't want me, so why should I want her?"

"Really, dude? That's how you feel? Shit, I'm not the one that's heartless, if you ask me. She is a bitch, though…and ruthless. Hell, everyone wonders where I got it from."

"No one wonders about you. And no one asked you for your opinion. So how close are we to getting those numbers I need. You got me some from Big Percy, but I still need the last pieces to the puzzle. And by the way, word is that Professor Timothy Carr is representing some people in the purchase of your old law firm. Any truth to that?"

"What? No, you must have gotten your signals crossed. 'He' did go there but only to get those numbers you need. Haven't gotten them yet, but a meeting has been scheduled and I will…I mean, he will retrieve them at that time. As a matter of fact, we should have them by the Gala this weekend."

"Gala? What Gala?" Vance asked.

"Oh, didn't I tell you? Part of my plan before we leave town is to attend the annual Christmas Gala that V puts on. You gotta bring Cassie as your date. I'm bringing Kerri. I just gotta make sure that Terri is too preoccupied to attend. I'm ready to cut V deep! I already cut Moms. Gotta keep it in the family."

"You know what? I'm just realizing how much you hate your family. Vengeance seems to be all that's on your mind."

"So? What's on your mind, Vance? The money...or maybe it's Cassandra? You've been spending a lot of extra time with her. Did you fall, brother?"

Vance just looked at his look-a-like and couldn't suppress a slight resemblance of a smile.

"Maybe," Vance responded.

"Maybe, my ass. Now, I know enough about transactions to know that it doesn't take weeks for money to move from one account to another, so I need you to get us plane tickets back by early next week. Monday would be nice. I think I've hit enough people but when I get these numbers and we hit the Gala, I believe I will have all I will need to feel vindicated and you should have all you need to make your move. I need to see everyone's face that hurt me, but we can't stay here for no chick...and especially not the one you're with. But then again, do what the fuck you want to do. I'm hitting and splitting."

"Okay, Vic. You're right and you're the boss."

"Damn straight!"

Victor smiled at that last statement. It had been a long time since someone stroked his ego and he missed it. Vance agreed with Victor, but he also had a change in his plans, as well.

CHAPTER 26

PLANS CHANGE

"Yes sir, Mr. Taylor, I'll get those papers together. Chase is bringing me the 'special' contract and will also sit in on the meeting."

"Good, Belinda. I would show up, but that would probably tip my brother on to what I'm doing. I trust you guys, though so, bring home the gold for me, okay?"

"No problem, sir. Now, you're sure you want me to give him these extra numbers?"

"Yes, but don't do it during the meeting. Do it on the sly, after the meeting. Victor came to get those numbers, but if you give them to him as if you felt it was something you were unsure about and it might prove useful to him, he won't have to make up an excuse to get you out of his office while he stayed in there and ruffled through your desk. I need his name attached to them for me to get what I haven't been able to get to all these years. You know I will make it worth your while, right?" V asked.

"I know, but for you, I would do it for free. But I'm like Arthur…I'm taking the money…I'm not stupid, you know?"

"Ha ha! Right! Anyway, just let me know when he has officially signed **all** the papers, okay?"

"Will do, Mr. Taylor. Oh, and Mr. Taylor? I hope your mother gets better."

"Thanks, Belinda. I believe she will…at least I hope so. Talk with you soon. Bye."

"Goodbye, sir."

As Belinda hung up, she was buzzed in by Lisa.

"Ms. Jett, Professor Carr is here."

"Okay, Lisa, I'm coming out. Let me grab my papers."

Lisa gathered up her important items and exited her office.

"Professor Carr! Nice to see you again! Ready to do business?"

* * *

V raced over to the apartment building where his people had said that Victor was residing. V told them to let him know where and when Cassie showed up. She did, so, he was in a hurry to catch them both in the act of being together and proving it wasn't him. Terri still hadn't talked to him since she viewed the tape and V knew it was time to fix this.

"Why Mr. Taylor? I thought I saw you come in already," the concierge said.

"You must have been mistaken. Oh, but I seem to have misplaced my room key. Could I have another one?" V asked, lying for a purpose.

"No problem, Mr. Taylor."

The concierge typed on the computer and another key was printed promptly.

"Here you go, sir. Have a nice day!"

"You, too," V said, while handing the man a $100 bill.

"Thank you, sir! Thank you very much!"

V didn't respond. He had already headed for the elevator to take him to 'his' room. It was on the 7th floor and located at the end of the hall. This particular hotel was catered to the slightly rich and almost famous. Each floor was painted a different color, but they all had gold trimming and their own separate continental theme. The floor V got off on had a light blue shade with scenes from Australia embedded into the walls themselves and the soft plush carpeted hallway, revealed sketches of koala bears and kangaroos. V reached his final destination; room 710. He stuck the key in and pulled it out quickly so that no one had time to respond. He found himself face to face with his brother.

"What the fuck? What are you doing here, Victor?" Vance asked.

"I'm not Victor; **you're** Victor!" V responded.

"I'm not Victor! I'm Vincent!" Vance lied.

"You can't be Vincent, fool! **I'm** Vincent!" V said.

"Stop playing, Vic! What are you doing here? Are you trying to ruin everything?" Vance whispered to V.

V looked at this man who looked just like Victor with a puzzled look, but kept his inquiry going.

"Where is Cassie?" V asked.

"She's in the bathroom. Why the fuck are you over here, Vic?" Cassie came out the bathroom.

"So, I was thinking, babe; maybe we could…oh! Victor?"

"No, I am **not** Victor! This motherfucker is Victor!"

"I am not Victor, I tell you! Cassie, I promise!"

"You're not Victor? Then take off that mask then!" V said.

"I don't have a mask on!" "It's true. There's no mask on him," Cassie interjected

"Then who the hell are you, then? I only have one brother and his name is Victor" V said.

"I'm confused," said Cassie. "I thought I was with Victor at first, but then he confessed to really being Vincent and now you're telling me that you are Vincent and I'm still with Victor? So, you're V, right?" she says to Vincent. "Now if you **are** V, who are you…especially if you're not Victor nor Vincent?" she asked, pointing to Vance.

"I am Vincent!" Vance lied.

"Okay, I'm tired of this shit. Who the fuck is Professor Carr?" V asked.

"Huh?" Vance replied.

"Huh, my ass! Professor Carr. Now I don't know exactly what you… you know what? Hold on a minute. I know how to get to the bottom of this."

V pulled out his phone and made a call to the firm.

"Hello, Chase? Are you in the meeting now? Okay, really quick; is Professor Carr there? He is? Okay, I'm calling back, but this time it will be to the firm. Inform Belinda."

Vance and Cassie just sat next to each other while V made his calls. She kept looking at Vance, wondering. Vance, at the moment, was afraid he would lose Cassie and he didn't want to do that, so instead of him making a move toward V, he was all into convincing Cassie to stay with him.

"Hello, Lisa? Patch me into that meeting and ask that Professor Carr talk on the phone. Tell him it's an emergency."

V waited for Victor to answer.

"Yes. Professor Carr, here."

V placed his phone on speaker.

"Talk!" he said to Vance.

"Hey, Vic. It's me," Vance said.

"Vance? Why are you calling me now? You know I'm in the middle of this meeting, right? I told you not to fuck this up and you call me? What's up?"

Vance had to think fast. Cassie was already looking at him with her mouth open, V soaked in the information and Victor was getting perturbed.

"Uh, make sure you get those numbers today. We really need them by tomorrow at the latest. Our window is closing."

"Don't worry. I'm getting the numbers **and** my firm back! Now, don't call me no damned more! Bye, fool!"

Victor hung up on Vance and now V was confused.

"Did he say, Vance? Okay, who are you really?" V asked.

"Yeah. I heard him, too…uh, **that** was Victor on the phone, right? He did say Vance., didn't he?"

Vance couldn't look Cassie in the eye, but he nodded.

Cassie continued. "He called you, **Vance?!**"

Another nod.

V didn't have to ask any questions; Cassie was doing all the work for him.

"So…oh, hi Vinny," she said to V.

"Hey, Cassie. How are you?"

"I'm good and you?"

"I could be better and I'm about to be."

"That's good. You got a plan brewing, don't you?"

"I do. You'll find out."

"Okay. So, if that was Victor on the phone, and **you** are really V, who the hell have I been sleeping with!? Who the fuck are you, motherfucker!? A fucking Vance?"

Cassie was pissed by now and you couldn't blame her. Even though, most times, she was the player; this time she felt played…and got played!

"You better talk fast, bro, before she grabs the Vaseline," V said. "Then it's your ass."

"Okay, okay. I come clean. Me name's Vancelot Evans. Last name should be Taylor, seeing as how me be part of triplets. Veenceent, I am

89

de brudda dat no one tole you boot. Hell, Victor dinna find out 'til he reached de islands."

V was stunned. *Another brother?* he thought. He would allow this **man** to finish, since he was so revealing.

"Go on," V said.

"Well, Vic and I come here to de states for our share of de money…"

"Wait a minute! You have an accent?! Where are you from?" Cassie interrupted.

"Jamaica. Sorry boot dat. I knew boot de money dat exchanged hands and I should have been involved and gotten me share, but no. Not de case. So, me come to get wot mine."

"So, what about Cassie? Why the video?" V asked.

"Video!?" Cassie asked. "What damn video!?"

Vance began to explain, not in complete detail, but enough to let Cassie and V understand what was going on and how Victor had revenge at the front of the plans. Vance hoped he wouldn't lose Cassie, and this was the only reason he was so forthcoming.

"So, you see, me dinna plan to fall in love wit nobody, but me fell for you, Cassie. You be de woman of me dreams."

Cassie didn't respond right away. A tear rolled down her face. She felt foolish and embarrassed.

"So, now what do you expect me to do? You pick me up so you can show Terri that her husband is unfaithful? Now that we know that's not true, now what do you expect of me? Damn, V…I mean, Vance, I've fallen for you, too!" she revealed.

V had sat back and listened to the whole story and had formulated his own plans.

"I've heard enough. I'll tell you two, exactly what **we** are going to do. Now you two can work out whatever you're going to work out, but before, during or after that happens, you will do as I say. It's either this or **neither** one of you will have what you want. No money; no love; not a damn thing!"

CHAPTER 27

Restored Order

It was cold, but there was no more precipitation. The snow had stopped falling and it was forecasted to return around Christmas. This proved advantageous to V and his Christmas Gala. There was enough snow on the ground already, but not enough to stop a party. Besides, this was New York, and no snow ever stopped a New Yorker. Since V was so busy this day, he kept calling the hospital to check on Moms; he kept calling Terri, but no answer and he kept calling his people that would assist him in his plans. He had to make stops to talk to important people. Even though he almost forgot, he had to make sure the Annual Christmas Gala happened as usual. It was the 22nd of December and this was how his friends, family and associates started out the Christmas season with a bang. He even made sure that everyone left with a gift…mostly an envelope with money in it. Chase always made sure there were enough envelopes. If 200 people were coming, Chase would have 500 envelopes…just to be sure he had enough. Each envelope contained $500, so everyone left in the Christmas spirit. V looked at the room that would be full of people later that evening and nodded his approval. He let the DJ in to set up and after that was over, he left to go pick up his suit for tonight.

"Seeing as how Victor will probably wear the same thing, I better make sure it's something he can purchase immediately," he said to himself. *No. I almost slipped up. Victor is expecting Vance. Better wear what Vance was going to wear.* V was sick and tired of this Victor fiasco, but was a little excited about the fact he now had another brother. He wanted to ask his father about it, but for some reason, 'Sabino' wasn't answering his phone. V decided to check in with Jr.

"Hey, man! What's up?" V asked.

"You would not believe what I found out!"

"About my shit?"

"No, about mine! I have finally gotten the tip I was looking for 4 years ago! And, dude, I'm sorry, but I've got to jump on this! Don't look for me to be at the Gala tonight."

"**What?!**"

"Calm down, V. I've briefed Pat and she will be there. You might think it's not the same, but it's damn near."

"Oh, so Pat knows you're home now?"

"Yeah, she had to. I popped in, hugged and kissed my wife and left. It seemed like she wanted to talk…like she had something to tell me, but I didn't have the time."

"Damn, man how are you able to read people like that?"

"Maybe I'm better than you think I am."

"Yeah. So, I'm just supposed to trust you about tonight, huh?" V asked.

"Yep."

"Okay. Done."

"Just like that?"

"Just like that. You've never told me anything I couldn't count on. Never. Besides, I'm going to have the Punishers show up just for coverage. You're my ace, and I know you wouldn't steer me wrong. Take care of business. Get the bad guy. I know **I** will."

"Yeah, I know you will, too. Look, I gotta go. I'll tell you all about it when I get back."

"You're leaving? Where are you going?"

"I'll tell you all about it when I get back, I said."

"Aw-ight, Jr. I understand. Be careful, dude."

"You, too."

* * *

"Damn, it's good to see you, man!" Sabino said to his guest. Sabino rarely has houseguests, so it pleased him that he could entertain at his house.

"Well, I'd rather be seen than viewed. Am I all set for tonight?"

"Yeah, I've taken care of everything. Even that special thing you requested. Are you sure about that?"

"I'm sure. I know what I like."

"Well, you have surely proven yourself. Ask me anything, and I'll get it for you."

"Good. It's time I showed everyone who's really in control. This shit has gotten out of hand and it's time to restore order."

"Restore order? Who's order?"

"Hell, everyone's! Even yours. You don't realize how much shit you're in, do you?"

"No. You want to tell me what I'm in trouble with?"

"In due time, my friend. In due time."

"Damn. I have a question; how do you know so much about so many people?" Sabino asked.

"Do you know Bill Gates or Jeff Bezos?"

"I know Gates, yeah, but not that Bozo guy."

"Be-zos. He owns Amazon. Anyway, those are two of the richest men in the world…known, that is."

"Okay, what about it?" Sabino asked.

"If they knew what I was worth, they would be jealous. I don't need or want anyone to know that I have become the first trillionare. You see, most people want to get rich so that everyone else can see what they have. It's all about showing off. Sure, I've made some expenditures that could draw attention, but when you have the kind of money I have, there's not much you can't do and believe me when I tell you; people most definitely can be bought. Tax collectors? Please. Money keeps them at bay and it's also enough that if they blew the whistle, their asses would be in trouble. I like nice things, but I don't care if anyone sees it or not. It's not about them…it's about me and mine! V almost has this figured out. That's why his new house is not so elaborate. It's a modest home, but it's big enough for his family and nice enough to enjoy for years. He's started his business and keeping things low-key. If you're going to be rich, don't tell no one. It's about the quality of life not the quantity of shit. There are a lot of unhappy wealthy people, so understand this; happenings do not equate to happiness. That is only found when you choose to be happy. And I'm quite happy…quite rich, too, but I had to understand that if were to be truly happy, money would not be the reason. I bet you can't guess what I want to do now, can you?"

"Probably not. What? Buy a yacht; the most expensive car ever; put someone out of business, start a business? Hey, I've got an idea! How about you advance me a bonus for my participation?"

"Okay."

"Okay? Just like that? Shit, do I say how much?"

"You can. It won't matter. If I like the number, I'll give it. If not, I'll give what I want."

"Okay, I'll take my chances. How about $100 million?"

"Hmmm…okay. Sounds fair."

"Are you shitting me? Really? Thanks, man!"

"No problem. Now what did I tell you I wanted to do? Do you know?"

"Hell, I don't know. What do you want to do?"

"It's Saturday, man! I want a good pizza, I want to find a good Western movie to watch and then nap until this evening! Think you can handle that?"

"Yeah, I can. I like you but you're strange, man."

CHAPTER 28

FINALIZATION

Kerri was admiring herself in the mirror. She had gotten special treatment, courtesy of Victor Taylor. Her nails were pristine, her hair and makeup were done by a professional stylist, and the dress that she had on would make the most beautiful of models jealous. It was a sheer black dress that showed off butt-hugging black shorts underneath. Its neckline plunged into the sharpest "V" you could imagine and the back just had two straps draping her in an "X". She wore a black diamond choker and earring set. She couldn't get over how good she looked to herself.

"Wow! I don't even recognize myself. I hope Victor approves…with his cocky ass! I sorta like him, but I really don't know what he's about. I do know he's got a little money, because he told me these were gifts!" she commented about her dress, jewelry and the other amenities.

"He's not bad in bed, either," she thought.

She looked over her shoulder in the mirror and smiled.

"Hell, yeah, he's gonna like this! I'm sure to get me some more of that 'D' tonight!"

* * *

"Are you nervous?" Chase asked V.

"To be honest, Chase…yeah. I'm a tad bit nervous about tonight."

V and Chase was at the Homer Towers where V's Gala was about to start. They had gotten there about an hour earlier to make sure everything went off without a hitch. Chase had his envelopes in a locked briefcase and keys to the different rooms to the building. He had proven to be a very good friend of V's, as well as an advisor. This endeavor tonight, however, would prove how well they would work together…in a conniving way. It was just about time to start the Gala. The DJ started playing his music.

"Well, don't be. You've got this. Everyone's in place and ready. You're ready…" Chase said.

"Am I?"

"Yes, I think so! You want this to be over, don't you?"

"You bet your ass, I do. Okay. No more scared-y cat attitude. Time for the tiger to come out!"

"That's it, V. Let's do this like Brutus."

"Yep. Can you hold things down until I get back?"

"I can, but where are you off to?"

"I have to go and pick up my date for the evening. When I get back, do not speak to me unless I approach you and don't react all crazy and shit. Be cool. Got it?"

"Got it. Wait! Are you picking up Terri!? You guys back together!?"

"It's a surprise. We'll leave it at that."

"Okay, then. I'll move when you move."

"Just like that!"

The men laughed and V made his way out the building. He didn't want to drive, so he used Uber. As he sat down in the car to go and pick up his 'date', he thought he saw Terri getting ready to enter the building. He started to get out of the car, but as he grabbed the handle, Victor walked up and she put her arm around his and they went inside. V just slumped back into the seat. He told the driver where to go. His heart was broken. *Damn*, he thought, *I can't believe I've lost Terri to that motherf… you know what? I'll play this through. I hoped he would come, anyway…just not with my wife. That's okay. It ain't over 'til it's over. Hell, let me make a call before I'm not able to.*

V pulled out his phone and dialed.

"Hello?"

"Hey, Pat? This is V."

"Yeah, I know."

"Say, are you still upset with me?"

"A little. Jr. says it wasn't you. I sorta thought that already, myself."

"It wasn't. Anyway, you still coming tonight?"

"On my way. I had to get pretty, too, you know."

"Hell, Pat, you're already gorgeous. Jr. is very lucky to be with you."

"Thanks, V, but don't be trying to butter me up to make me like you right now. You know what, though? There is something you can do to make all of this better!"

"What's that?" V asked.

"You say that's not you in that video?"

"That's right."

"Prove it."

"That's exactly what I'm doing and I hope to finalize this by tonight!"

CHAPTER 29

UP татат SPEED

Victor mingled among the crowd, not pretending to be anyone but himself. Kerri was right there with him, on his arm. At first sight, everyone thought it was V and Terri, but when Victor let on as to who he really was, everyone that knew the story was shocked to see Terri with her ex-husband. Victor was eating it up and he couldn't wait until V saw him with his wife's double. It was a point of his to make sure that **everybody** saw him with this woman. His plan worked; people started talking. *That's not V! Victor is with Terri! Oh, shit wait until V finds out!*

Chase had already had his conversation with Victor and he knew something was up because Victor was in too good of a mood. He knew it wasn't V, but then Victor never let on that he was anyone but himself. Chase watched Victor while drinking at the bar. He couldn't drink too much; he had to be conscious enough to complete a task, if asked to. Lisa had finally made it and he had to apologize to her for not picking her up.

"I had to be here early, babe," he offered.

She said she understood, but deep down, she was still a little miffed. She was now helping Chase by being on the lookout for V when he returned. Neither she nor Chase knew who V was talking about when he said date, because they were viewing who they thought was Terri.

"I don't get this," Lisa said to Chase.

"Don't get what?"

"I don't get this Victor shit. How is it that he's strutting around with Terri and she's just acting like nothing happened?"

"I know, right? It doesn't make sense, but V must know about this already. But he said he was picking up his date. It sure the hell ain't Terri."

"Did you call him?"

"Not supposed to. We'll wait it out. V's our friend, but this is his problem. Whether he knows or not, he'll handle it."

Kerri walked up to the bar where Chase and Lisa were seated and ordered a martini.

"So, Terri, are you enjoying your and V's party?" Chase asked.

"Oh, so is that what you guys call Victor? V? He never told me that. Oh, and by the way, my name is not Terri."

She grabbed her drink and walked away from the couple. It was probably a good thing she did; they were speechless anyway.

* * *

V made it back to the function, with date in tow. When he walked in, he was the center of sorrowful looks and half-hearted hugs. The people didn't know how V would take seeing his wife with Victor, but they were surely surprised to see V with his ex-girlfriend, Cassandra. The talk started all over. *Oooo. The shit is fixing to hit the fan! V's with Cassie; Victor's with Terri! Oooo!* V and Cassie walked in hand in hand and V, after seeing Victor across the room with 'Terri', tried to put on a good front of being happy and tried his best to keep a smile on his face. What he hoped for now was for Victor to finally see him. He couldn't actually let on to the people that he was not there in the person of Vincent Taylor, anyway. This time he was...

"V! You made it! Hello, Cassie." Victor saluted.

"Hello, Victor. Hi, Terri."

"My name is not..."

"Important at the moment," Victor interrupted. "Excuse me for a moment."

Victor pulled Kerri off out of earshot and discussed the current situation.

"Kerri, we agreed or did you forget? You would play Terri just long enough to make my brother mad, jealous and hurt and when this is over, I'll set you up. Tonight, you are Terri. Got that? You're not reneging on me, are you?"

"No. I just keep forgetting to answer to Terri. I got it now. No worries. But if that's what you wanted, shouldn't he be throwing a fit right about now? Looks like he's with who he wants to be with."

"That's not V, baby. V hadn't made it here yet. That's Vance, my other brother. I can't say that in front of Cassie. She thinks it's V. Talk about someone not staying in touch with current events. She doesn't even know V is married to Terri now! She still thinks I am! Head must've been stuck up her ass for four years."

"Ha ha! That's funny, Vic. Okay, I'll be good now, but can I be bad later?"

"If you're talking about what I hope you're talking about, hell yeah! You want some more of this, huh?"

"No. You want some more of this!" Kerri said, turning her backside to Victor.

"Shit, you ain't never lied."

They walked back over to V and Cassie.

"Say, Cassie, can I borrow your date for a minute?"

Cassie was doing all she could to control her breathing. First of all, she was at this party, part of a deception and second of all, she was finally standing right in front of who she thought she would be with all along… Victor Taylor. She certainly still had feelings for him, but she just now realized they were not like the ones she had for Vance.

"Sure," was all she could barely get out.

Victor and V walked away from the ladies.

"So," Cassie started, "how are you and Victor's son doing?"

Kerri just looked at Cassie like she was crazy. She knew nothing of a son. *That damn Victor did **not** catch me up to speed on all this shit!* she thought.

* * *

"So, Vance, are you ready? I have the contracts and I think you'll be pleased to know that I have some additional important numbers and forms for you, as well. I was informed that without my signature, this account could not be opened. Did you know this already?"

"Yes. I did," V said, truthfully. Vance may not have known, but V wouldn't let on he was not the other brother…not yet, anyway.

"Okay, I'll forgive you for that. Especially if this is the jackpot we came here for! I have my firm back, oops…I guess you were right about that. I've got those papers locked up already. You won't need them. Oh, well. We'll have a shitload of money and V's, Terri's and Moms' heart will be broken! I'll tell you, brother, I thought I wanted revenge, but when I found out what could be dropped in our laps, my thoughts were refocused. Hell, fuck that, I most definitely still want revenge. That's number one! Have you seen V yet? I can't wait to see his face when this all hits!"

"No, not yet."

"Okay. Let me know when you do. Here. Take these numbers and hold on to them with your life! I've signed the forms, so all you have to do is…"

"I know what to do."

V was starting to grow agitated at Victor and the jealousy and pain that Victor wanted to inflict, were being made evident in V's psyche.

"Okay, damn, you don't have to get all huffy and shit. Go back to your date and let me get back to mine."

"Alright. Oh, before you do, I need you to sign a couple of more papers and then we are rolling! This will speed things up. It's sorta like priming a pump. Oh, and here's a little starter for you in this envelope. Do you like, say $1 million in a cashier's check?" V said.

"Sure the hell do! You got a pen?"

V hands Victor a pen.

"Anything to finish this up," Victor said while signing. "By the way, she looks just like Terri, doesn't she?"

V reacted uncontrollably, but tried to play it off.

"What? What do you mean, looks just like Terri? That's not Terri?" V asked.

"Naw, man, I already told you! That's her twin sister, Kerri," Victor said while walking away, stuffing the envelope in his jacket.

V stood where he was, looking at the spot where Victor was just standing as if he was looking right through everyone and everything. Slowly, but surely, a smile broke out on V's face. He stared in the direction of Kerri. She was as beautiful as he imagined Terri would be and all he could think about now was his wife. His spirits were lifted.

"No wonder she didn't act like she was mad to see me with Cassie! That chick doesn't even know Cassie! Hell, she doesn't even know me!"

CHAPTER 30

#StayWoke

Vance couldn't stay in the hotel room he shared with Victor. There were entirely too many emotions and thoughts whirling around in his head and he had to get out. Seeing as how almost everyone that knew Vincent would be at the Gala, Vance didn't see any trouble in going to the hospital. He didn't really know Moms and he didn't have any emotional ties with her, but she was his biological mother and he felt maybe he should just go and check on her. Since she was still unconscious, he didn't see the harm. He just knew he had to get out of that hotel room. Thinking about Victor's plans; what was Cassie doing; if they would wound up with the money they planned on; all these and more had Vance juiced, so maybe a nice visit with someone who couldn't talk back would be appropriate. He put the address of the hospital in his Waze app and when he made it there, Vance made his way towards Moms room and was flooded with even more thoughts and questions.

Why did she give me away when I was born? Was I uglier than my brothers? That can't be it…I look just like them. Did she not have enough love for three? Hell, does she even know I exist?

He opened the door to her room and looked in before he entered. He saw this woman, who seemed to be resting peaceably. The room seemed to give off the smell of an eco-friendly cleaner. The sheets on the bed were pressed and the floors sparkled like new glass. Vance was surprised she wasn't hooked up to anything…not even an IV. He walked over to the side of the bed and stared at her face, trying to see the resemblance of himself in her. Vance noticed her beauty, even though age tried to hide it. He had never had any reason to have feelings for this woman…but for some reason, he did. Like it or not, she was his mother…and to him, she was beautiful. Vance was so entranced with his mother that he didn't even notice the door opening and another visitor coming in.

"Hey, V."

Vance was startled and looked up at the face of Terri.

"Hey. What are you doing here? I thought you'd be at the Gala," Vance said. At first, he thought it was Kerri, but then decided it best he not say anyone's name…just in case.

"Yeah, I was just about to ask you the same thing. It is still going on, isn't it?"

"As far as I know. Are you okay?"

Terri kept her distance. She didn't come any closer than when she first walked in the room.

"I'm getting there. You look skinny," she said.

"Well, that's probably because I'm not making rational eating decisions."

"That's probably true. I guess you blame me for that, huh?" Terri smiled at knowing how true that really was.

"Well…"

"So," she continued, "any changes with Moms?"

"Not that I know of."

Just as Vance answered that question, a slight buzzing of an alarm started going off beside Moms hospital bed. Moms twisted her face, opened her eyes and reached over to grab the alarm to cut it off. She yawned real big before realizing she had visitors. She saw Terri first.

"Terri?" Moms asked.

Terri moved quickly to her bedside.

"Moms! Hey! Welcome back!" Terri had tears streaming down her face. She was scared, so she couldn't control her feelings. Vance looked at Terri and couldn't figure out why.

"Girl, I've **been** back. Been woke all day. Shoot, I stay woke! Even when I'm sleeping. I couldn't figure out why no one was here to visit me, but I knew what today was. Even told the hospital, if anyone calls, tell them 'no change'. I may have been down and I may have been out, but I heard all kinds of talk. As a matter of fact,… V?" Moms looked over to her right to see Vance. She turned back to Terri.

"Why aren't you two at the Gala?" she asked Terri.

Terri and Vance looked at each other and both shrugged their shoulders.

"Well, I didn't know you or anyone else was coming to see me tonight, so I already made plans. I'm going," Moms said.

"Going where?" Terri asked.

"To the Gala! Where else could I have been talking about?"

"Home," Vance said.

"Yes, I guess you're right about that one. But you're wrong about that one. Get it? Terri, could you reach in that closet and grab my clothes for this evening?"

"Sure, Moms, but do you think you should be getting out of bed so soon? You need to build your strength up, don't you? You have to be released and all of that!"

"Girl, I told you; I've been up all day. I've already taken care of that. As a matter of fact, I'm already released. I've walked the halls and had a great lunch. They just let me stay until I got ready to leave, so I could get me some rest from all that sleeping. People will allow you to do some crazy things when you make a donation, huh? It's crazy how sleeping for days can make someone tired, too."

"Wow! So, you're going to the Gala?" Vance asked.

"So, do you want us to take you? We could take her, couldn't we, V? We should be there, anyway. It's our function."

"Uh...yeah. We could drop you off."

"Drop her off? No, V, we are going to take her in. Okay, Moms?"

"Okay," Moms said. "Terri, could I have a moment with my son...in private?"

"Sure, Moms. I'll be right outside. V, come and get me when you guys finish talking and I'll help Moms get ready. By the way, this is a pretty dress, Moms."

"Thank you, baby."

Vance just nodded at Terri. She left the room and Vance was face to face with a conscious mother.

"Come here, son. Let me look at you."

Vance leaned in.

"Come closer."

Moms held his face between her hands. She looked in his eyes and pulled on his ears and cheeks. She squeezed his nose for good fashion.

"Hmph! No mask," Moms said.

"What? I don't wear a mask. What do you mean? Why does everyone assume I wear a mask?"

"Don't worry about it." Moms released his face, but never took her eyes off of him.

"Now, son, I'm going to ask you a question. Would you lie to your mama?"

"My mama? No, why would I?"

"Uh huh. I think I know why you answered that way. So, let me ask you another question and I want you to listen to it real well. Would you lie to your own mother?"

"Uh…I would like to think that I wouldn't lie to my mother. Again, what reason would I have to lie?"

"I don't know why you would, but you already have. You have a scent about you that connects you to me. I smell you and I can tell you're mine, but you're not Vincent because he would have reacted a bit more with love and excitement when he knew I wasn't in a coma and also, even though he cares about me, he's too responsible to not be at a function that he is sponsoring. You're not Victor because that ass wouldn't visit me in the first place and he's probably the reason I'm in this predicament. You're distant yet familiar. You haven't even spoken my name since you got here…maybe because you don't know what to call me. I raised two boys and I know my sons by their eyes more than their looks **and** I know what my sons' eyes look like, but I've never seen yours before. There's a kindness and compassion in them that I haven't seen in my other two boys. There's no doubt that you are a splitting image of those two, so you must be their brother. Which means, I don't know how, but you're my son, too. There's more wrongs going on in this family that I care to count. Now, here's your chance to prove to me that you would not lie… anymore, to your mother; that is, if I **am** your mother and you know I'm your mother. So, my main question is this: who are you and what are you doing here?"

CHAPTER 31

ACT ONE

Jr. boarded the plane with a ticket to Bora Bora. He would fly to LAX in six and a half hours, and then layover there for four and a half hours before heading to Tahiti. This would be a long trip, but he hoped it was worth it. This time, he was in disguise. He wore black corduroy pants, a Camel skin coat and a multi-colored toboggan. On his face, he had a long salt-and-peppered beard and matching moustache. He wore shades, even though it was night. He looked like an old, Black hippie that was stuck in the late 60's. He got on board and placed his carryon in the bin above his head. He sat down, put on his seatbelt and watched the other passengers come on board. He was looking for someone in particular. He had seen him before, but even with that, he had a picture to help him to pick him out when he entered. Jr. purposely purchased a ticket that sat him towards the back of the plane. It didn't take long before his target made his way down the aisle to claim his seat. Jr. made note of this man. Black leather jacket; black leather baseball cap; gray button-down collarless shirt; skinny blue jeans, Ray Ban prescription glasses that darkened in the sunlight and lightened inside buildings. He sat about six rows in front of him. Now, all Jr. had to do was sit and wait until they landed…and not lose him. Only then, would he be able to make his move. He just hoped that his intel and info was correct or else, Jr. would look like a fool. He trusted his source. The plane started to fill up and Jr. was seated in an aisle seat. He needed this in case he had to move fast. The stewardesses all got into position to act out the procedures of flying or in some cases, crashing. No one wants to be prepared for that. Jr. watched the presentation and then put a stick of gum in his mouth to help his ears to keep from popping. He then set an alarm on his watch to wake him up an hour before they landed in Los Angeles. He thought he'd get a nap. He asked for a pillow and blanket and kicked his head back.

Well, well, this should be the break we've been looking for, Pat, he thought to himself. *I'll make sure you get some credit behind this.*

* * *

The DJ was playing everyone's favorite. Even though V had other agendas, he noticed that it seemed like everyone was having a good time. Even Victor got out on the dance floor…with Kerri. Of course, if V had not been made aware of Terri's twin, it would have pissed him off to see who he thought was his wife dancing with his brother. He smiled again, but he had to remind himself that until things were finalized with his plan, he had to stay in character. When Victor handed V the papers and numbers, V had to find his way over to Chase, without Victor being the wiser.

"Here, Chase. Take these and go upstairs. You already know where, so let me know when you finish," V said.

"I'm gone, boss. Say, are you alright?"

"Yeah, why wouldn't I be?"

"Victor is out there with Terri. You came here with Cassie? I'm confused."

"Don't be. You'll be caught up eventually. I'm good."

"Are you sure?"

"I'm sure. Thanks for your concern, but I'm fine."

"Okay. So, this will work, right?" Chase asked.

"Hell, I'm not the one that works the figures! You are! You tell me."

"Yeah, okay. It'll work. It's all about punching the right numbers and you can trust me on this. I'll get it done. Have your phone handy."

"Text only. Will do. Waiting on you."

Chase walked away and headed for the hallway to get on the elevator. He made double sure that Victor didn't see him so he included Lisa in the plan.

"Hello, Mr. Taylor! Remember me?" Lisa asked Victor, while he was at the bar ordering drinks.

"Lisa? My old secretary? Hey! What the hell are you doing here?"

"What do you mean? Oh, you didn't know. Mr. Taylor...uh, the other Mr. Taylor, has been putting this on for years now. I've always come."

"I see. So, who are you here with? Didn't I see you with Chase Morton?" Vic asked.

"Yeah. He came over and spoke to me. I think he likes me," she lied.

"Yeah, I felt that. I talked to him earlier. Seems he's not with the firm anymore. Shame."

"Why do you say that? Doesn't he deserve to do what he wants to do?"

"Sure, he does. It's just that he was a pretty good attorney, that's all. He was making a name for himself. Kinda reminds me of myself. Besides if I ever were to run a firm again, I would want him on my team" Victor said, smugly.

"Well, from what I hear, he's still making a name for himself...just not in the judicial field."

"Oh, really? What field is...you know what? Never mind. If the money is right, he'll come back. Well, I must say, I'm glad I came tonight. This is really a nice shindig."

"It's good to see you having a good time. I've never seen this side of you before."

"Well, it's easy when you're celebrating."

"You're celebrating? Celebrating what, if I might ask?"

"You may not. That's none of your damn business. If I ever want you to know something, I'll tell you. You should already know that."

"Oh, sorry."

"No need to be sorry. Like I said, If I wanted you to know, I would've already told you." Victor took a sip of his drink. "I bet you're thinking I haven't changed much, aren't you?"

"Well, Mr. Taylor, there's one thing for sure. You certainly are still as smart as ever."

With that, Lisa walked away from Victor. He watched her from behind.

"Welll! I knew she was a little smart-assed bitch," Victor said. "Nice ass, though. Hell, that's why I hired her." He headed his way back over to Kerri.

This conversation Lisa had with Victor was just enough for Chase to ease out and make his way upstairs. All players playing their parts.

CHAPTER 32

THE INQUISITION

Terri drove her car straight to the Gala and Vance followed in his car. Moms rode with Vance, because she didn't want Terri to be suspicious as to who this stranger might be. Neither one changed clothes; except Moms, of course. She had on a nice sequined forest green gown and a tiara with an emerald in the middle of it. She had on long gloves that came up to her elbows and she wore diamond bracelets. She would always be festive when she went to this event, and even though she didn't quite feel like being that way, she would muster up the strength to try. She felt that this was a good time to question her driver.

"So, it seemed that the cat had your tongue back at the hospital. So, I'll ask you once more; what is your name, son?" she asked.

Vance was quiet. He just kept his eyes on Terri's car so he wouldn't be separated from her.

"Oh, so you're not going to talk at all, huh? That's okay. I'll talk. You listen. Boy, I don't know what you have in mind for me and my family, but I'll warn you: you have come up against the wrong people. I have another question for you: is Victor in town?"

Silence.

"Uh huh. You're silence tells me what I need to know. So, you and Victor are in this thing together, huh? That's alright, don't answer me. I'm going to get down to the bottom of this eventually. I now know it was Victor who sent me that tape. His fingerprints are all over it. Probably literally, but for sure figuratively. So, he's trying to hurt people, huh? Well, you can tell him for me, if I don't get a chance myself, that he did hurt me. He hurt me bad. But you know what? It wasn't he who deceived me in the first place. I just can't believe V didn't tell me. I'm a little pissed off at V, but I'm sure he had his reasons. Even though I don't know you all that well, I'm surprised you didn't stop Victor."

Moms stopped talking and the interior of the vehicle was silent for a few moments.

"Me name is Vancelot. People call me Vance. Last name Evans. From Jamaica. Me parents were Dr. Joseph and Mrs. Mary Evans. Dey took reel good care of me. Brought me up right. Me knew aboot Victor and Veencent, but me was no jealous. Had a good life. Found out aboot dis money dey where coming into, and me lost me mind. It seemed only fair, since I was de one who got de ball rolling. Me didn't come here to hurt nobody."

"Damn, son, you have an accent, don't you? Joseph and Mary, huh? Like in the Bible?"

Vance laughed.

"Yah, me guess so."

"Wait a minute! Did you say, Dr. Evans?"

"Yah, ma'am."

"He was the doctor that delivered my babies!"

"Yah? He never tole me aboot dat."

"Is he still alive?"

"No. He die aboot tree years ago? Me mom died two years before dat. Both of cancer."

"Aw, I'm so sorry to hear that. Well, I'm not trying to replace anyone. You were born from me, but raised by her, so…your real father is still alive, too. Bastard!"

"Huh?"

"Nothing. You'll learn soon enough."

"Okay."

"So, you met Victor? He came here to hurt people though, didn't he?"

"Yah, ma'am, he did."

"So…is he at the Gala?"

"Yah, he is."

"And Vincent is there, too?"

Vance nodded as he turned the corner following Terri. Moms smiled.

"Shit, this is going to be fun, son." she said.

"You really tink so?"

"I really do."

"If you say so…Moms, is it?"

110

"Yes, sir. Moms it is."

* * *

The drinks were pouring; the music was thumping; the people were having a good time. Victor was whirling and twirling Kerri out on the dance floor as they danced to Step in the Name of Love. V just kept watching the door, waiting for Chase to reenter. The doors did open, but it wasn't Chase that came in. It was as if the music was planned to play for the individual that entered. The song was the Isley Brothers', "Superstar" and in came this man, dressed to the nines, with a gray and black Chinchilla fur coat and a matching fur Fedora. Underneath that, he sported a dark blue Michael Kors suit, a light blue Robert Graham edition shirt and two-toned blue and black Steve Madden shoes. He wore a $130,000 gold Rolex with a diamond incrusted face that twinkled like the stars in the sky. At times, it seemed to blind a person. He donned a $300,000 bracelet that was completely covered with sapphires and diamonds. You would think a person who wore such exquisite attire would fear of someone jacking him, but nothing but confidence exuded from this tall man. Walking in front of him on a chain was a Black panther with a collar that matched the stunning Rolex. He wasn't a full-grown cat; he's what you might call a teenage panther. When the people saw it, they started moving back out of the way. They didn't care if it was full-grown or not; it was a panther. Walking in beside this man, was Sabino. They walked in like they owned the room. The music didn't stop playing, but the people stopped dancing…just to look. They wanted to see what fool would bring a panther to a party. If he wasn't a fool, he must be a boss that flossed! V noticed him right away and recognized who it was. He made his way over to him, forgetting that he was supposed to be Vancelot. He didn't even give any thought to the panther.

"Kev? Is that you?" V asked, while shaking his hand.

"Nope. This here's the Colonel!" Sabino offered.

Kevin Casey winked at V. They already knew.

"No worries, Sabino. He knows who I am."

"Oh. Well, let me go and check on the servers and the food. Moms is not here and I sorta took over for her. If she ever finds out it didn't go well, she might be mad."

"Okay, Tony. I'll see you later," Casey said.

"Damn, it's good to see you! What brings you to New York; or should I even ask?" V said.

"Good to see you, too, V. It is V, isn't it?"

"Yeah, it's me. Do you need to test me to make sure?"

"I'm too careful not to. When's the last time you saw me personally?"

"At the airport when I met your ex-wife, Pat's mother."

"Okay. Unless you told someone about that, it's you. I had to be sure. Is my daughter, Pat here?"

"Somewhere. She's sorta on duty. She might be hiding in a corner or something or she went to the bathroom. I don't see her now."

"Well, I'm sure I'll see her before the night is over. She's gonna need some reassuring, you know."

"Yeah, I know. Wait. No, she won't. She knows."

"She's in on it?"

"Yeah, she already knows. She's ready."

"Cool! Well, that's one thing taken care of."

"Why do you say that? Wait a minute! Is that a damn panther?"

"Yes, it is! His name is Samson. Hadn't lived up to his name yet, but he will."

"Shit, I'm just glad it's tamed. He is tamed, isn't he?"

"To a degree. There's always going to be some wild side in him. Kinda like you and me, you know?"

"Yeah, I guess so. Look, I better get away from you before Victor notices. You know who I'm supposed to be, right?'

"Yep. I know. That just happens to be another thing taken care of."

"What else do you have in mind?"

"You shouldn't even have to ask. I'm about to squash all this shit that's been going on."

"All of it?"

"All of it!"

"Well, then call me when you need me. I'll be over at the bar."

"Cool. I'll find a seat over in the corner…that is, until I'm ready to make my move. Come on, Samson."

The Colonel and his cat sauntered across the floor to a seat that Sabino had reserved just for him. He took a seat, had someone bring him a drink and watched as the show began.

CHAPTER 33

FAMILY REUNION

Terri and Vance pull up to the Gala and park their cars in the garage of the building. Vance gets out and walks around the car to open it for Moms to get out.

"Well, one thing's for sure; you're certainly not Victor," Moms said.

Vance smiled as he helped Moms out of the car.

"Okay. Let's get in here and find out what's really going on."

Terri reaches out and grabs Vance by the hand. As far as she knows, this is V.

"I'm sorry I've been so mean to you. I guess I owe you the chance to explain, huh? We'll talk. Okay?" Terri said.

"Uh…sure." Vance replied.

They all walked into the room together only to be met with eyes of surprise. People started walking over to Moms, telling her how good it was to see her up and about. V noticed the commotion and ran over to her. Victor was still drinking and dancing; he hadn't even noticed when the Colonel came in. But now, the party people were confused. They were seeing three identical looking men.

"Moms! What are you doing here? Are you okay? Wow!"

"I'm good, son. How are you?"

"I'm g…" V stopped mid-sentence and noticed Terri holding his other brother's hand.

"What the hell are you doing here?" V asked Vance.

Vance just shrugged his shoulders. He knew part of the plan was for him not to be there. He was just as tired of all the charades as anyone else and he was also tired of answering questions.

"Why are you asking him that, Victor? This is his function! He should be here!" Terri said.

"Terri, dear," Moms interjected, "that's not Victor you're talking to. And the man's hand you're holding; that's not V. That's Victor out there," she said, pointing to the dance floor.

"What? I'm confused," Terri said.

"Join the club, baby. Now, this young man standing in front of us is V. Victor is on the dance floor. And this man here is…" Moms said.

Cassie walked up and put her arm around V's arm.

"What's going on here? Moms!" Cassie let go of V and hugged Moms. "It's so good to see you! When did you get out?"

Terri started fuming again.

"Tonight. I could've left earlier, but I left when I did. Why are you here with Vincent?" Moms asked.

"Oh, this isn't Vincent, Moms. That's Vincent," she said, pointing to Vance. Vance shook his head but didn't want anyone else to see.

"This is…" Cassie finally noticed that Terri was standing right next to Vance.

"Wait a minute! I thought you were already here!" she said to Terri. "As a matter of fact, who is that dancing with Victor?" Cassie asked.

Everyone's eyes concentrated toward the dance floor and saw Victor dancing with someone who looked just like Terri. The authentic Terri started moving towards the scene as if she was sleepwalking.

"Wait a minute! If that's Terri out there with Victor, then who is this with me?" Moms asked, while looking at Terri, then back to the dance floor.

"Let me try to explain…without fully explaining. I'm Vincent and this is Cassie. Terri, I'm not really with her tonight, but I'll have to tell you about that later. This individual in front of us is Vancelot Evans. He is Vic's and my brother. That is Victor on the dance floor. That lady on the dance floor with Victor is Terri's twin sister, Ker…"

"Kerri?" Terri said, slowly making her way towards her sister. V got the DJ's attention and gave him the 'cut it' sign. The DJ stopped the music and Victor and Kerri stopped mid-step. They looked up and saw Terri moving their way. Kerri moved towards her twin until they were face to face. Victor stood back and began grinning.

"Kerri?" Terri asked, this time to Kerri.

"Hey, Terri. I've been looking for you."

"Have you? You've found me, sis. I'm right here."

The sisters hugged and tears streamed down both of their faces. Everyone witnessed the event, but V was just glad that Victor was not with Terri. He had already surmised that, but now he had to explain to Terri what he was doing with Cassie; the same person he was accused of sleeping with! Moms held onto Vance, just in case he thought about sneaking out. Victor was just smiling; pleased with the mess he created. He didn't like how the sisters got along so well, so fast, but he still felt like he had caused discord in the family as a whole. Moms looked up and saw Sabino come out of the kitchen area. She made a beeline towards him, but she never let go of Vance.

"Come on!" she said to Vance. Moms was on a mission.

"Elaine! You're here! When did you…?"

Whack! Before Sabino could finish his question, Moms had slapped the man as hard as her strength would allow her. Sabino was crouched over to the side he was directed and slowly brought his head up.

"You bastard! How could you? I thought you loved me? You couldn't have! Damn two-timing Negro!"

"Elaine. Let's not do this here. Let's go somewhere private and talk."

"Why do you want to go somewhere private? You did all of your shit out in the open; let's keep things that way! Bastard!"

Vance stayed close. Even though this was not the woman who raised him, it was the woman who gave birth to him and he felt a protective spirit come over him. She didn't have to hold on to him anymore…he was holding on to her. He held her back in case she wanted to do more than just slap. He didn't know if she was strapped or not. V and Victor came up to the ruckus.

"What the fuck is going on?" Victor asked, very well knowing, trying to contain his joy.

"You know what the fu…, you know what's going on, Victor! This is my supposed to be dead husband! Only thing is, the bastard is not dead! Ooo, I oughta kick your ass, Thomas!"

"Moms, calm down…" V said.

Moms turned to face V.

"No, V. You do not have the right to tell me to calm down! I'm mad at you, too! Why didn't you tell me?"

"Moms, I'm sorry. I couldn't. Besides, he promised he would either leave town or leave you alone and he didn't do either. I am so sorry."

V put his hand on Moms shoulder, hoping she would forgive him. Moms looked him straight in the eyes.

"You hurt me, son."

A tear rolled down both Moms and V's face. It hurt him that he hurt his mother. Moms took her hand and wiped the tear off of V's face.

"I am so sorry, Moms."

"I know. I'll get over it eventually. But right now, I'm beyond pissed and I'm about to open up a can of whoop ass on somebo…"

Moms turned back to where Sabino was, only to find him to have disappeared in the crowd.

"Where did that bastard go? Did anyone see where he went?" Moms asked.

Everyone was clueless and the people that happened to be standing close by, tried to stay out of it. Sure, there were the nosy ones…but they eavesdropped only momentarily and out of respect for Moms, they moved away from the situation. Everyone; except for one person who seemed to gravitate towards the situation.

"I know where he is. When he's needed, he'll show up."

"Who are you?" Moms asked.

"The name's Casey. Kevin Casey. Most people call me the Colonel."

"Well, Mr. Colonel, ain't no soldiers around and you don't tell me what to do! People call me Moms and it's not because I'm so motherly."

"Moms! The Colonel is here to help. Don't be so…"

"Boy, don't you tell me nothing right now. I'm pissed! If I had my strength, I'd probably turn this whole party out!"

"Ms. Taylor, I understand you being upset, but if you will just follow me, I will clear everything up for everyone. As a matter of fact, all of you should follow me…even you, Victor," said the Colonel.

"No. Especially you, Victor," V said.

CHAPTER 34

IN CONTROL

The DJ cut the music back up and the party was back on only this time it was missing some of the attendees. The Colonel had everyone involved in this mess to meet in a conference room nearby. V had all the keys to the building, so getting in was not a problem. Everyone followed him to the room, he unlocked it and then left to go find Chase.

"I'll be back in a minute. I have to take care of something," V told the Colonel.

"That's fine. This will take a few and I'm not in a hurry. I'll see you when I see you."

"I'll be right back."

Everyone started filing in the room, but Moms grabbed Victor and held him back so she could talk with him in the hallway.

"So, Victor Taylor. How've you been, son?" Moms asked.

Victor just gave her an evil grin.

"Yeah, I know it was you that sent me that video. Do you hate me, Vic? Did you want to hurt me that bad?"

"I should be asking you the same damn thing. You hurt me, or don't you remember. You lied and I had to leave. Remember that, Mama? See, as long as it benefits someone else, it's okay, huh? Fuck that. Yeah, I needed to see you hurt. Didn't know it would put you in the hospital, though. You're just a tough old bird, I knew you wouldn't die. I sorta hoped…"

"You sorta hoped what, son? That I did die? You know what, you used to be a pussy of a boy and now you're a pussy of a man! If I had the strength, I'd knee you in the balls! I wish I didn't love you right now, but I can't help myself. You're my flesh and blood; my first-born son; my heart. But I swear you are a lowdown bitch of a man and I am not unhappy about saying it. Just like you came back to cause havoc to everyone, you would not have been a good fit to stay in the first place!"

"Moms? Kiss my ass!"

Moms tried to slap Victor, but he caught her hand before it reached his face. He expected it to come.

Victor grinned again, turned from Moms and then went inside the room to take his place at the table. Moms hurt him again with her words, but he still felt vindicated with the hurt and division he caused between her and V, as well as the riff he caused between her and his father. He saw Kerri sitting on the far side of the table right next to Terri. Kerri was towards the front of the table. He went over to sit next to Terri.

"Excuse me?" Terri said.

"Oh, sorry about that. Got you girls mixed up. Ha!" Victor lied.

"Like hell you did! You know I didn't have on an outfit for tonight!" Terri responded.

Victor moved on the other side and sat next to Kerri, trying to keep from laughing. She and Terri were trying to catch each other up with their lives, but they knew they would have to table this conversation for another time in the short future. Moms came in and sat down on Vance's left and Cassie, who was sitting on Vance's right, was holding onto his right hand with her left. They were situated across from the twins and Victor. The Colonel sat at the front end of the table and just sat there looking over everyone.

"Say, man, can we get this shit started and over with?" Victor asked.

"Patience, Victor. It'll start shortly. It won't end fast enough for you," the Colonel responded.

Victor gave a puzzled look back to him.

The door opened and V, Sabino, Patricia and Chase came in. Pat had stayed out of sight earlier, and she missed everything that went about on the dance floor. V was right when he said she might have had to go to the bathroom, because when the events with Terri and Kerri happened on the floor, that's where she was. V had Alphonso and Marco to stay with the party to make sure everything continued as it was. Sabino went and stood on the wall behind Victor; Chase sat down in a chair with a seat between Cassie; and Pat stood on the wall just inside the door behind Moms. V went around and sat next to Terri. She just looked at him for a moment and then turned her attention back to Sabino. He tried to reach out for her hand, but she slowly snatched it back in her lap. Victor noticed and grinned again. As far as he was concerned, everything he put in motion was coming to fruition. Before the Colonel began the meeting, Pat recognized her father.

"Daddy? Daddy, is that you?" Pat asked.

"Hey, baby. Yeah, it's me."

Pat left her post and rushed over to Kevin. She gave him a big hug and she couldn't control the tears that ran down her face. He returned the embrace, but held back the tears.

"Oh, Daddy! I didn't know you would be here! It's been so long!"

"Yeah, I know," the Colonel said. "How've you been? And that husband of yours…how is he?"

"He's good. Busy, but good."

"I know."

"You know? How do you…you know what? Never mind. You're the Colonel, right? You know shit we probably don't know, right?"

"That's right, hon. Let's chat later. These good people are probably ready to go home. Am I right?" he asked the group. They nodded. Pat went back to her post and stood ground.

"Okay. Did everyone have a good time at the party? You got a good DJ, there, V. It doesn't matter, though. As good a time as some of you had in that room back there, some feelings are going to get hurt in this room here tonight, that is, if they aren't already. I'm going to be doing most of the talking, because I know most, if not all of the information…about everything. You could say that I'm in charge now."

"Everything? You know everything?" Victor asked.

"Yep. Everything," the Colonel answered. "So, where do I start? Well, let's start with Ms. Taylor and Mr. Sabino, okay? Hell, almost everyone in this room knows, but since it's not 100%, I'll let you two have the room when we finish. Is that okay with you, Ms. Taylor?"

"That'll be just fine, kind sir. I need to be alone when I say what I have to say to that mother…, to Mr. Sabino over there."

"Good. So, let's move on to the next few items, mostly caused by our friend, or should I say, enemy, Mr. Victor Taylor. You have come back to the states to make everyone's life a living hell, am I correct? Revenge, correct?"

Victor just looked at the Colonel and grinned.

"You seem to be pleased with the way things are going right now. That's quite alright if you don't answer. I know every damn thing you tried to do. It was you who staged the sex scenes with Cassie and your other brother, Vancelot and it was you who delivered the damaging tape to Terri, hoping it would break her heart and then break up their relationship. Am I right so far? Yeah, I know all about it."

Victor never responded…just smiled.

"I also know about the tape you sent to your Mother. You're heartless, you know that? I wish I had known this about you before. I never would have included you in my plans. I can't say that what I've done is completely legal, but I haven't intentionally hurt anyone. But you? Wow. You're a mean motherfucker. Excuse my French, ladies."

"Well, may I say to you, Colonel, fuck you very much!" Victor said.

"Wow," was all the Colonel could get out.

"Excuse me. I remember you. Officer Casey, is it?" Terri interrupted.

"It was, but please…call me Colonel."

"Oh, okay…Colonel. Can I ask a question to my husband?"

"By all means. I've got nothing but time."

"Thank you."

Terri turned to V.

"V. I found it hard to believe that was you on that tape. I did for a minute, though because the times you were supposed to be with Moms or in a meeting, it was the same times you were on that tape! That hurt, dude. Now if you weren't really there in that room with Cassie, where were you? And who was that?"

"Terri, I'm sorry. The Colonel already told you that was Vance, there. I meant to tell you the day after Moms catering job where I really was. You were so tired that night and to be honest, I was a little scared to share with you what I did. I probably shouldn't have been. We've based our relationship on trust, so I don't know why…" his sentence trailed off. "A friend from high school called just as I was helping Moms and needed a favor with a car…"

"A friend? Female friend?" Terri asked.

V was emoted. "Yeah. Took me all day to fix it, but I didn't want you to think I wasn't doing what I said I was doing, especially while you stepped in for me at the business. Nothing happened between us. I really didn't have anything to tell, I just didn't tell you everything, that's all."

"So, what, you like her or something?" Terri asked.

"Well…I used to in high school. I didn't do anything against our marriage, Terri…that is, except not be totally truthful."

"So, what about tonight? Why did I see you with Cassie?"

"Just for that bastard on the other side of you," V motioned towards Victor. "I am not with Cassie. As you can see, she's with him," he motioned to Vance. "I love you and only you, Terri. You gotta believe that."

"And do you two remember why you couldn't reach each other? Your phones were out of whack, remember?" the Colonel interrupted.

"Yeah." Terri and V both nodded. "I know I tried several times," Terri said.

"Mr. Vance, here, hacked your phones…on both occasions. He's pretty talented, you know. He's what's known as a super hacker."

"That brings me to another question: who are you again and where did you come from?" Terri asked, looking at Vance.

All eyes fell on Vance as they waited for his response.

CHAPTER 35

SUPERIOR BEINGS

"His name is Vance," Moms offered.
"No, Mudda. Allow me," Vance said. "Me name's Vancelot Evans. It appears me be dose two's brudda. We be triplets and Victor met up wit me on de island of Jamaica. Dat's where me be raised by two kind folks. Me only came here wit Vic so dat me can get what me feels me was cheated out of. You know me be right, don't ya, Casey?"

"Yeah, man. I apologize. I truly forgot about what you did to set this off. I promise to make it right with you," the Colonel answered.

"Well, anyway, me met dis girl 'ere," as he pointed to Cassie, "and tings changed. Me tink me in love. No, me sure of it!" He looked at Cassie, but she couldn't return her eyes to his.

"Well, well," said the Colonel. "I really hate to be the one to bust your bubble there, bro, but while you thought you were playing her, Ms. Cassie was also playing you. You see, she was in cahoots with a guy named Roger. Right, Ms. Cassie? I think you already know him, don't you, Vance?"

"Yes. If it's de same Roger me know."

"He's your photographer, right?" the Colonel inquired.

Vance nodded. The grin slowly left Victor's face.

"Say, is that the same Roger you brought to Moms dinner years ago?" V asked.

"That's the same one, V," the Colonel answered for Cassie.

"Wait just a goddamn minute! How do you know so much about who is…or what…what…whatever?!" Victor asked.

"Man, when you have as much money as I have, you can have just about anything. I'm not bragging, I'm just saying. I'll tell you. I have my own satellite…and I'm not talking about satellite TV."

"What?! How the hell did you get a satellite?" Vic angrily asked.

"I contacted someone at NASA, told them what I could pay them and they built me one. Sent that bitch up into space and connected it with me. Victor, I know everything."

"Shit." Victor said.

"So, wot is dis aboot dis Roger fellow?"

"Well, he and Cassandra here plotted to get information from you so that she and he could run away together…with your money, no doubt."

Vance looked at Cassie with disbelief.

"Is dis true? You play me?"

"I'm sorry, Vance, but yeah…at first, I was going to. When Roger found out I was back with…well, I thought it was Victor, he had a plan. At first, it was all about the money. I was running away, but not to be with him. But I fell for you, too, baby. I told Roger I was out and I didn't care about no money. He didn't care if I was out or not. He said that he had other plans."

"Oh, yeah? Well, what about that $222 mil promised you?" asked Sabino.

"That was you guys doing. I didn't come up with that number and I was put in a position of doing what you told me or else. I had no choice."

"Well, did you do what you were asked to do?" Sabino asked.

"Yeah. And I gave those numbers to V. You really gave me no choice."

"Wait a fucking minute! Shit, it's just hitting me! Vance? That's you across the table from me? And this is V beside Terri? All this time tonight, I thought I was talking to Vance and I was really talking to V? V, you got my damn numbers?"

"Afraid so. You see, Vic, you were so careless after you left the states. You dropped your guard. Had you read the contract you signed, you would have known that you could come back to the states a little after a year. But you didn't read it, did you? Naw, you're too damn smart for anybody else. But you see, I needed you to come back because I couldn't touch quite a bit of money. The bank is located in Jamaica and I was going to share it with you for your troubles, but now…shit, son, I'm taking all your shit! All of it!"

"Not all of it. I'm not telling you everything because I still don't believe you know it all. You neither, Casey."

"That's cool. I don't give a damn if you believe I know it all or not. Just for that, I'll let some of this shit that's going to roll off of you be a surprise. You see, I have so much money I can do just about anything I want...except find a way to keep from dying."

"You seem to be proud of yourself for having so much damn money. You can't stop saying it," Victor said.

The Colonel's phone rang and he answered it. "Hold on a second. Hello? Yes sir. You got him? Red-handed, huh? Good job, agent. Bring him home and chill with your wife for a while, okay?"

He hung up and looked at Pat. "That was my son-in-law...your husband."

"My husband? Jr.?"

"Yes ma'am. He caught that Roger dude. Seems he took my formula, added two more ingredients and came up with a product he could ship undetected, but his shit had the same criminal contents that cocaine does. It still wasn't coke, but it certainly was illegal. He bought a ticket to Bora Bora, but he tried to dump his stash and himself off in California. Never intended on going all the way to Bora Bora. Good thing somebody tipped off Jr., huh?"

"Yeah, somebody," V said, smiling.

"So, Ms. Taylor, like I said earlier, I guess you already knew by now that Victor sent you that tape, right?" the Colonel said.

"Yes, I know. My boys...hell, and their damn daddy!"

Moms eyes pierced at Sabino. He just dropped his head.

"So, V, what did you do with my numbers? That's my shit, son!" Victor asked.

"Mr. Chase Morton, here took care of that little matter. Right, Chase?"

"Yes sir, Mr. Taylor. You now have access to your $3 billion dollars. Sorry, maybe I shouldn't have said that out loud," Chase said to V.

"No, no, that's fine. And thank you, kind sir," V responded.

"You bastard! You can't get away with this! How much of that is mine?" Victor asked.

"Not a damn dime, now! You fucked up, brother! Coming back trying to hurt everybody. That's bullshit, Vic. You wanted payback, but now you will have to pay back," V said.

Victor jumped up out of his seat. Sabino put his hands on his shoulders and sat him back down.

"Sit down, clown!" Sabino said.

"What? You mad? So, if you had gotten away with what you tried to do, it would be alright? Like I said, you fucked up, Vic. You came up against not only your equal, but your superior!" V said.

Victor was steaming and he knew he couldn't do anything about it. He did tell himself, however, that at least he got his firm back. That was a contract he perused **before** signing and it was legal and binding. Those papers he still had.

Vance was in a stupor. He didn't know what to believe about Cassie so he thought he'd ask.

"Cassie. I love you. D'yuh love me?"

"I do, Vance. Really." They kissed.

"How sweet," the Colonel said. "Get a room. Okay, is there any more news that anyone would like to share?"

"Yes, I have something," Kerri said.

"Why, yes of course. You haven't spoken all evening. Would you like to introduce yourself first?" asked the Colonel.

CHAPTER 36

KARMA

"Sure. Hello, everyone. My name is Kerri and I'm Terri's twin sister…"

"Kerri, uh…?" V asked.

"The last name doesn't matter to anyone here. What matters is that Terri and I were separated when we were six years old and I always wondered what happened to her. I missed her tremendously so I started looking for her. I know you won't believe this, but I met someone down in Louisiana and he told me that I looked just like someone he knew. It was your husband, Pat. It was Jr. and he told me that I could probably find her in New York. I guess he was teasing with me, because he was just about to tell me exactly where she was and all of a sudden, he was rushed off by some other guys in dark suits and shit. Hell, we didn't even get a chance to exchange numbers or nothing. Well, I've been in foster homes all my life; some bad; some not so bad. I'm a grown woman now, but I never really thought about trying to find my sister…that is until Jr. said what he said. So, I headed out to find her and wouldn't you know it, she found me."

She squeezed her sister's hand.

"I missed you, Terri."

"I missed you, too, girl."

"Why didn't you look for me?"

"Yeah, and you never mentioned her," V said.

"To be honest, I got news from a cousin down south that you were killed in a car wreck. Girl, I cried and cried that night. I was married to Victor then, so he didn't think anything of it. He thought I was upset with him…hell, I probably was that, too!" Terri said.

"Well, sister, I believe you. Someone did die in a car wreck that night and I was thrown from the vehicle. It was my car, but I wasn't driving and when the car hit the eighteen-wheeler, it caught on fire. I was thrown and the girl driving was burned to death. No one looked for me because they thought that was me, seeing as how she had on a dress she borrowed from me."

"Aw, hell, what a touching damn story," Victor said, uncaring.

"Oh, and one more thing; Victor? I realize that everyone seems to be coming at you from all sides and I'm not one to try to add to your dilemma. You do need to know something else about me, though. I'm pregnant."

"So? What're you telling me for?"

"You're the father, you bastard! Don't get embarrassed by taking a DNA test. You are the only one I've been with in the last six months and as of yesterday, after a little visit from a local gynecologist, I am pregnant with your child. It doesn't take but once, right?"

"Oh, shit, you talking about some karma!" V said, laughing.

"Shut the hell up, V!" Victor said.

"Oh, my God! Are you telling me I'm having another grandbaby?" Moms asked.

"Yes ma'am, if this is your son," Kerri said.

Terri and Kerri hugged.

"Well, I'll just be damned," Victor said. Sabino was beaming, knowing that was his grandchild, as well…that is until he caught Moms eye again. He stopped smiling and dropped his head.

"Congratulations, Ms. Kerri! You, too, Victor," the Colonel offered.

"Fuck you!" Victor responded. The Colonel laughed.

"So, is that all?" the Colonel asked.

"That's all from me," Kerri said.

"Okay. Are we finished here?" the Colonel asked.

"I'm afraid not," said Cassie.

"Oh, I'm sorry. Please. Go on."

"Well, there's two things I need to get off my chest. One is, I'm pregnant, too."

Gasps filled this room as if everyone was searching for breath.

"That one ain't mine!" Victor exploded.

"I didn't say it was," Cassie answered.

"Wha? Whose baby do it be?" asked Vance.

"It be your baby, Vance. I'm no whore. I don't just sleep around with anyone. At first, I thought you were Victor, coming back to claim me and then you told me you were V, coming back to claim me. I wasn't sleeping with Roger…well, I did once four years ago; but that was the only time. He sucked at sex! He and I were business partners and that's all. I wasn't sleeping around and I really was waiting on Victor to come back around, but he didn't…and I'm glad he didn't. I'm glad it was you, Vance. You gave me true attention and I could see in your eyes something I never saw in any of your brothers' eyes. Sorry, V. Vance, I love you so much and I would like to make a go with you…that is, if you'll still have me."

"Yes, baby, me still won you bad! You say dose tings to me, I be filled up wit hope and love."

"Good, I am so glad to hear that. But that might change after this second thing I need to get off my chest. My goals were to get that money and run away with you, Vance. But it seems other people have changed my plans. Colonel? You said you're rich, right?"

"Beyond your wildest dreams."

"But you're pretty much off everybody's grid, right? If something were to happen to you, not many people would take notice, huh? Many wouldn't even know, would they?"

"Tis true. I'm not much into notoriety. I just like the life I live."

"So, you said that you could do just about anything you wanted to do, that is, except prevent yourself from dying, correct?"

"That is also correct. Why all the questions?"

"Oh, just curious, that's all."

With that being said, Cassie pulled a .22 caliber pistol out of her clutch and shot the Colonel in the chest. He fell back onto the floor and blood gushed everywhere. Everyone went into some type of action. Pat moved quickly and grabbed Cassie from behind while Vance took the gun out of her hand. Pat pinned her to the ground and placed handcuffs on her. V and Sabino had gotten to the Colonel and was trying to plug up the hole where the blood was coming from. Vance was now consoling Moms and the sisters were huddled together on the floor. Chase was in shock. The sound of the gun caused him to push back from the table and it seemed as if he was stuck to the wall he had made it to. He could not move from where he sat. Victor was also still seated, but not because of shock; he was brooding and didn't care.

"Chase! Chase! Chase, wake up!" V called out to him.

"Huh?" Chase said.

"Call 911! Hurry up!"

Pat got Cassie up to her feet. She looked at Vance.

"I'm sorry, baby, but he took what was ours."

Vance couldn't speak. He just held onto Moms.

"Everybody! Get out of here! You do not want to be here when the EMT's and police come! The least you know, then the least you can tell someone. Go back to the party or go home. Get out, now!" V barked.

Everybody started filing out except for V, Sabino and the Colonel. As Victor walked around where they were on the floor, he looked down at the scene.

"That's what you get, motherfucker! Call yourself taking my shit. That'll teach you. Thanks, Cassie!" Victor said, as he pimped out of the room. Chase was the last one to leave.

"Chase. Close the door behind you, okay?"

Chase couldn't talk. He just nodded and closed the door.

When everyone was clearly gone from the scene, V spoke.

"Okay, Kev. Everyone's gone. You can get up, now."

"What?!" Sabino said.

"Are you sure everyone's gone?" the Colonel asked.

"I'm sure. You can get up."

"What the hell is going on?! Colonel? You're okay?" Sabino was clearly clueless.

"The Colonel baked this one up! Cassie, Pat and myself were in on it. We couldn't let too many people in on it, or it wouldn't be believable."

"Help me up, boys."

Sabino and V helped the Colonel to a chair.

"Damn, that hurt a little more than I thought. Like I said, when you have the type of money I have, you can get just about anything you need. I had this bullet-proof vest made with compartments which holds fake blood. She's a good shot. I had a medallion on the spot where she needed to hit and I'll be damned if she didn't hit it. V, I'm glad you trusted her. She could've aimed for my head!"

"Yeah, and she wouldn't have missed, either. I used to take her to the gun shop and let her shoot until she got good."

"I can't believe this! You're a genius!" Sabino said.

"I guess. Naw, I can't take the credit on this one. V, come clean. You know this was your idea. Fess up."

"Okay," V said, shyly.

"Hell, now I can be dead to the world and continue living it up. I will keep in touch with Pat, though."

"All I have to say is, thanks, Kev…for everything." V said.

"Naw, man, once again…thank you. Now help me get cleaned up and out of here. Oh, and make sure you grab my cat!"

CHAPTER 37

NO SENSIBLE ANSWERS

"Hey, Moms! Say, let me put something in your ear."

V was running down Moms to tell her something. He had already secured another meeting place for Moms and Sabino to hash out their differences. V had another brainstorm.

"Hey, Moms, I know you're getting ready to talk to Daddy, but I want to run something by you."

"The Colonel? Did he...?"

"Yeah, Moms. He's gone."

"Damn, that's too bad. He seemed nice...in a controlling type of way."

"Yeah, that was him. I want to run something by you."

"What's that, son?"

V leaned over and whispered in Moms ear until he had finished what he had to say. Moms leaned back and looked at V incredulously.

"I'll consider it, V. Just for you."

"Not just for me, Moms. Not just for me. For everybody...even for you!"

She smiled and hugged her son and then went to the room where Sabino was already waiting.

When she walked in, Sabino had his head in his hands and he looked like he lost his puppy.

"Hey," she said.

"Hey, there, Elaine."

"Why are you sitting here moping?"

"You're kidding, right? I know you're going to tear a hole in me. I'm prepared for it."

"Oh, you think you know me, huh?"

"I used to."

"Well, I thought I used to know you, too. Tell me; did you know about my other son?"

Sabino looked away.

"You know what? Don't answer that just yet. Take off that mask first."

"What?"

"Take off that mask…Thomas."

Thomas Taylor took the mask off and looked at Moms with tired eyes. He was tired of masquerading as someone else and he was tired of lying to his 'widowed wife'.

"Damn, Thomas! You have no idea how much I've missed you, do you? Why? Wait, tell me about my boys first."

Thomas went about explaining what happened when the boys were born. When he finished…whack! Moms had slapped him again only this time as Thomas and not Tony.

"You're gonna have to stop doing that, Elaine!"

"Why is that? You gonna do something to me?"

"No, it's not that. That shit hurts!"

"I meant for it to. Now, Thomas…you kept one of my children from me. You may not have thought we could have made it, but to sell one of my boys because of what you thought, was selfish and childish. Vance was my baby, too and I deserved the opportunity to raise my son. Do you see how stupid that was of you?"

"I guess, but…"

"You guess?! What do you mean, 'you guess'? Hasn't this hit home to you yet?"

Thomas got quiet for a minute.

"Yeah, E, it has. It wasn't the same for me back then. We were barely getting by and we knew we would have to make provisions for twins. But triplets? I wasn't ready for that."

"And you think I was? I didn't even know. It wasn't our fault we didn't know. We went on what we were told. Even if it was one more mouth to feed, don't you think we would have found a way? Don't you think other people might have helped? Not that I would have counted on that, but, Thomas, you never gave us a chance. Why, Thomas? Why did you choose the money over me and the boys?"

"I really can't answer that. I loved the boys...and you...still do. I was in shock and for some reason, it seemed I would be in trouble if it looked like I was responsible for Sabino's death. So, Kevin Casey convinced me that things would be better for all if I portrayed Sabino and let Thomas Taylor die. I don't really have a sensible answer for you. I guess I got caught up."

Moms just looked at him.

"I was talking about the first amount of money you took for Vance."

"Oh. Hell, I don't know. It hit me all of a sudden. We were okay after that, you must admit, right?"

"Financially, sure. I didn't know where you got that money. Didn't even know how much. I just knew you were making sure we had what we needed. I thought you were being mature and responsible. I know different, now."

"Look, E. I am so sorry I did what I did. I thought I was getting paid and we would wind up the better. I can see now that it was really I who paid a terrible price."

"I wondered why I was so attracted to Sabino. I had never seen anything before in that Italian that I liked, but the way he moved lately caught my attention. Hell, I should have known. I must say, you were pretty good at being him."

"Uh, thanks? I am so sorry, Elaine. What can I do to make it up to you?"

"Well, V has an idea he wants me to run past you."

"Okay, E. I'm listening."

* * *

The people started leaving the party and many shook V's hand and thanked him for putting on such a fun and fabulous affair. No one heard anything from earlier, except the little tiff on the dance floor between Moms and Sabino. No one asked any questions. We're talking about Moms and Sabino, so it's probably best to not question what happened. They were all glad that they were able to get out and enjoy themselves. After the DJ finished packing up his equipment, he walked over to V who handed him an envelope. He didn't have to look at it. V had never shorted him in the past and so it never crossed his mind. He gathered up his stuff and left the building. V looked at the door that everyone had just left out of and sighed a big sigh. Unbeknown to him, Terri was across the room watching him say his goodbyes to everyone. When he turned around, he caught her eye. She motioned with her pointer finger to come to where she stood. He made his way over to her, almost as if it took everything in his body to fight the gravity that was trying to hold him still. When he reached her, she looked in his eyes.

"When you said what you said back there, you were telling the truth, huh?" she asked.

"I was."

She looked even more deeply.

"I believe you."

"Thank you. I've missed you so much."

"I know. I've missed you, too…and Vas."

"Right. Are we a family again?"

"We are…we really never stopped being one. But we still have to talk. Agree?"

"Agree, baby."

"Oh, and by the way, did you taste the orange juice tonight?"

"Yes, I did, and might I say, it was the shit!"

Terri smiled, kissed her husband and held him just as tight as he held her.

CHAPTER 38

R. I. P.

V opened his eyes, yawned and stretched his arms toward the sky. He rubbed his eyes to make sure he wasn't dreaming. There beside him, fast asleep, was his wife Terri. It felt good to wake up in the house that you and your spouse built together, but even better than it being their house, it was their home. V and Terri spent some much-needed makeup time last night, so V was doubly happy. He looked up at his ceiling fan that was running on medium and he could feel the cool breeze blowing against his skin. He looked over at his walk-in closet and could make out a few of his favorite outfits to wear, as well as a few shoes on the shelves. He could smell the remnants of the incenses he burned last night in the bathroom of a combination of Jasmine and Sandalwood. Yes, he was back home. His best friend Jr. would be coming in this afternoon and it would be good to see him, as well. V certainly had a story to tell him and was also certain he would hear one, as well. V got up and went to the bathroom. He took a leak, washed his hands and then his face, brushed his teeth, grabbed a robe and then headed to where his son Vas would be sleeping. He stuck his head in his son's room and just looked at him. *I missed you, son,* he thought. He didn't want to wake him. After the weekend that everyone just had, they all agreed to sleep in this Sunday. He was thankful to God, for sure, but he wouldn't be in attendance today. It was too early to call anyone…except one person. *Hell, I'd better take a shower, first,* he thought. So, that's just what he did and after his shower, he put on some sweat pants and a T-shirt and then went to the library, closed the door behind him and picked up his cell.

"Hello?"

"Hey, Colonel? How's it going?"

"Great, V! And yourself?"

"Man, right now it's pretty fantastic! Did you already make it home…wherever that is?"

"Yep. Me and Samson arrived early this morning. Sorry I couldn't stay last night. My plane was on standby and my pilot was well-rested. Besides, I'm dead, right?"

"Right. Man, that was some performance last night, huh? Now if only Cassie can keep her mouth shut."

"Think about it, V. There was no evidence of a weapon found; there was no body to take out, so if she says anything now, she will really go to jail…and for a long time, too! It's for her best interest to stay silent."

"Yeah, you're right. I just thought I'd give you a call. You know I won't bug you, right?"

"V, you can call me anytime you'd like, okay? There's always an open line for you. So, have you talked to Pat at all?"

"Yeah. She's pretty bummed."

"But she understands, right?"

"She says she does. Do you think you could arrange for her to come see you sometimes?"

"Man, I can arrange anything I want. Are you asking for her or for yourself?"

"I guess I'm asking for both of us. She's been a really good friend of mine and you already know she's a great daughter. She doesn't deserve to go through the rest of her life miserable about her father. I mean, she knows you're not dead, but shouldn't she be able to spend some time with you? Don't you agree?"

"I do. You're right. Tell her not to worry and that I'll make it happen soon. Okay?"

"Okay. And thanks again for your help. Say, I do have one more question?"

"Ask."

"Big Percy. Is he really dead?"

"Afraid so."

"Did Victor kill him, because I know I didn't."

"I knew you didn't. Nope, Victor didn't kill him, either."

"I hate to ask this next question. Who did then? Did you kill him?"

"Well, not literally. You see, Big Percy worked for me all along. You remember catching me passing papers to him in prison, right? Hell, I know you didn't know what it was about, but I couldn't have you saying anything to anybody. As you very well know, too much was at stake. Percy was very important to us getting ours. A true computer wizard. But he messed up. No real fault of his, but again, I take no precautions when it comes to me and mine. When he saw Victor at the prison and thought it was you, he gave Victor some important info that should have never gotten out. When I talked to Percy, he understood he jeopardized things and took the pill we arranged for him to take if it ever came to this. He just wanted to make sure his mother was taken care of, since Victor didn't come through like he promised. He also told me he was tired of living that prison life, so he thanked me for an easy and painless way out. It's almost like he looked forward to that day. I've already set his mother up."

"So, he poisoned himself? He didn't feel any pain?" V asked.

"None at all, bro. Took the pill, went to sleep and kept sleeping. But now, I have to hook your other brother up. I swear I forgot that dude, but I'm going to make it up to him. When you see him, assure him of that fact."

"So, what did Vance have to do with all of this?"

"Hell, when I met Vance over in Jamaica, he was trying to follow after his 'father'...you know, the doctor that raised him. Vance had excelled in school with a Major in Medicinal Chemistry and an Minor in Computer Science. He was already established in his field when I got there. He was on vacation at the time and we started talking. I don't know why I confided in him so, but I told him I slipped up on a discovery, but I knew that the ingredients I was using would get me in trouble. He said he'd look at it further and see if something could be done. Boy, was something done! Vance came up with the correct proponents that made things the way they are! Can you believe after all of this, I forgot this dude?"

"Kinda hard to believe."

"Yeah, well if it hadn't been for your brother, Vance we never would have gotten this thing off the ground. I'll tell you this, too...if you find a way to use him with you, do it. You won't regret it. Please tell him I got him, okay?"

"Will do. Well, Kev, it appears I can hear my family waking up. I better let you enjoy your "deceased state of being". The last thing I want to do is blow your cover. I'll call sometimes...but, only if I need to."

"You better do it more than that. Take care, V. Oh, and by the way, you are one smart cookie. All these ideas and plans; man, their yours. You did good."

"Thanks, man. So, did you. Bye."

"Bye, V."

The men hung up their phones, knowing in their hearts that the other man would be just fine.

* * *

It was now midday and Sabino had stopped by for a cup of coffee with V. He could also see his grandson while he was there. Most everyone involved knew who he really was…except Vasyl. V and his father decided to keep it that way.

"So, did Moms go along with our idea?"

"Don't you mean, your idea? Yeah. She's down. Thank God. I should really be dead, you know?"

"Yeah, probably. You better be glad Moms has a good heart."

"So, what about you and Elaine? You guys good?"

"It's a process, but I think we'll be alright."

"Sounds good. So, V. When I got the Colonel out of that place on the sly, did the EMT's and police still show up?"

"Yep."

"What happened?!"

"Well, I had already talked to the PD and the EMT's earlier that day and worked everything out. No one was really paying attention as to how many men went in, so one of them got on the gurney and they covered him and zipped him up before they came out. They never arrested Cassie because they knew there was no one guilty of a crime. Sure, they put her in the back seat of the squad car so that everyone could see, but then they took her to her apartment. Pat got the gun, so they never found a weapon…hell, they never looked for one! This was mainly done to get back at Victor, but he still doesn't know it yet. He will soon, though. Revenge? Hmph! I'll show him revenge."

"What you got planned now, V?"

"Naw, I can't spoil the surprise, but you'll be here when it happens, won't you?"

"You little punk, you."

"Aw, flattery will get you nowhere."

"So, this evening then?"

"This evening, Dad. For sure, this evening."

CHAPTER 39

BEE-OTCH!

Victor was packing his clothes for the trip back to Jamaica. His flight wasn't until tomorrow, but he didn't want to wait until the last minute to get this task done. Vance was sitting in the chair, staring out into space.

"Say, man, get up! Aren't you going to pack?"

"Wot for?"

"To go back home, dude! What do you mean?"

"I can't believe dat Cassie would do such a ting," Vance said, shaking his head.

"Hey, she's a woman, ain't she? Shit, I'm glad she did. I wish I had a gun. I'd a shot him in his goddamned head!"

"Yeah, well me don tink me gwine anywhere."

"What?! You're staying?! Why?!"

"For Cassie. She be needing me and I'll be 'ere for 'er. Besides, she's carrying me baby."

"Man, how do you know that bitch wasn't lying about a baby. And who's to say it's really yours?"

Before Victor could react fast enough, Vance was up from his chair and had Victor by the throat, planting him against the wall.

"She's not a beetch! Take it back or you won be needing dis neck! I'll snap dis muddafucker!"

"Okay! Okay! She's not a bitch! She's not a bitch! Damn! Let me go!"

Vance let go of his brother's throat and Victor slumped to the floor, rubbing his neck, choking. He had never realized Vance's strength until now. Vance worked out.

"Now, de next time you say someting aboot Cassie in me earshot, me gonna fuck you up real bad like! Understand?"

Victor couldn't speak at the moment, so he gave Vance a 'thumbs up' with his free hand. Vance's phone rings and he answers. *Ya'll both bitches!* Victor whispered.

"Hallo. Yes, Veenceent. Me believe we can…no, me knows we can. See you den. Goodbye."

Victor had picked himself up to a sitting position by now, rubbing his neck.

"That was Vincent? What did that bastard want?"

"We have been invited over to Jr. and Pat's house to discuss…issues. 5 pm. We're gwine."

"I'm not going around those motherfuckers anymore! I'm through with their asses! I'm taking my firm and going back to Jamaica…without seeing them anymore!"

Vance walked up to Victor while still in the chair. He leaned down and got right in his face.

"You know wot? You and me, we been true a lot togedder, yes? We have spent the last four years getting to know one anudder, true? I tink you are a stinkin' bastard, but I also have come to accept your ass de way you be. Sometimes, I even like you. Not much, but sometimes. I'm gwine to say dis so, you will understand me better and dere be no miscommunication between us. Okay? Brudda…we…are…going!"

* * *

Pat was on the phone at her house.

"Now, remember, Cassie. Don't contact Vance until you hear from us, okay? We need to make sure Victor is long gone first…if he even leaves."

"Oh, he'll leave, alright," Terri said in the background. "My sister is having his baby and Victor does not want to be around a baby."

"Did you hear that, Cassie?"

"Yeah, I did. I'll lay low and wait for you guys to call me," Cassie said.

"Alright. Bye, now."

Pat hung up and Terri gave her that condescending look.

"Why are you looking at me like that?"

"Girl, you know I don't trust that heifer!"

"I know, but she may be changing. Vance has affected her. She's not chasing after V anymore, so you should be happy."

"Well, I still say I will only trust her as far as I can throw her."

"Well, don't be throwing her anywhere. She's with child, child."

Moms stepped in the room. "Hello, ladies."

"Hi, Moms," they both replied.

"Look, I was wondering if I might have a word with Pat…alone, that is."

"Sure, Moms. I'll be in the kitchen, Pat."

"Okay, we'll be in there in a minute. Right, Moms?"

"Oh, this won't take long, dear."

"Okay, see ya'll in a minute," Terri said, "Pat, I have had many a conversation with Moms in this bedroom, so…"

"Girl, if you don't get out of here," Moms said, playfully hitting Terri on the butt. Terri left for the kitchen and Moms started in.

"Sooo…" Moms said.

"Sooo, what, Moms?"

"Sooo…"

"Moms! What is it? What are you trying to say?"

"Oh, nothing. I was just wondering why you didn't tell everyone last night that you were pregnant, too."

"What? I'm not pregn…"

"Pat, I was born at night, but not last night! I've been around the block a couple of times and I know the difference between someone getting fat and someone that's pregnant. You're not getting fat, but you are gaining weight. Now, you're pregnant. Aren't you?"

Pat plopped down on the bed.

"Yes ma'am. I am. You can tell? How?"

"I can tell. Okay. Why didn't you share?"

"I wanted to tell Jr. before I told the world. I'm not so sure he'll be happy about this."

"Jr.? Girl, yeah, he's gonna be happy! He better be! I've put up with just about all the shit I'm gonna put up with these men, so he **will** be happy!"

"Moms, you're crazy. You won't tell anyone, will you?"

"Moms is the name and mums is the word. Don't worry. I won't spoil if for you."

"Thanks, Moms. You know what? You're kinda special."

"Yeah, some might say that. Ha ha! All I know is ya'll been doing a whole lot of screwing here lately!"

CHAPTER 40

HERO

"Say, man, thanks for picking me up. I'm sure glad that's over!" Jr. said to V.

"Are you sure you're glad? You know you like this shit."

"Love it, but still that doesn't mean I'm not glad it's over. Do you realize it's been over 4 years solving this case?"

"Yeah, I know. You know, I could've been the bad guy, seeing as how I was involved with the Colonel and his 'feel good' drug."

"Yeah. Would've busted your ass, too."

"You would not! At least without giving me a head start at getting away, right?"

Jr. didn't answer. He smiled.

"Right, Jr?!"

"Yeah, yeah, you're right. Damn, man don't be so emotional. You know I love you like a brother."

"I hope so. You're my real brother, too."

"Yep. Man, I can't wait to see Pat! Thanks again for coming to get me."

"No problem, dude. So, you caught the bad guy, huh?"

"Yep. I had to watch his ass when we landed in California, because he didn't seem to be trying to stay in the airport. Saw him get on the phone and then headed towards the luggage area. He must've already set it up for his shit to stop there, even though he had a ticket all the way to Bora Bora. You can't throw this dog off no scent."

"I know that's right. So, his stuff was packed how?"

"He had that shit sewn into the lining of his suitcases."

"If it couldn't be detected, how did you know where to look?"

"Hell, I didn't really know. The Colonel knew, though. He told me. How he knows all of this shit baffles me."

"He has his own satellite."

"He has his own what?! Well, I guess that explains it."

"Yep. So, go ahead and finish with your story."

"Okay. I sat close enough to him on a shuttle bus, took my razor, cut the bag while he wasn't looking and 'accidentally' dropped my bottle of water where some would fall in the cut. By the time we reached our stop, that shit was oozing out. When he realized what was happening, his ass started to run, so I shot him."

"You shot him?!"

"Okay, not really. Just thought it would help the story. No, I shot in the air. Everybody hit the ground, including him. He was smart enough to know he may have been smuggling drugs, but he didn't want to die. I even saw his pickup vehicle. Got the license plate numbers, called it in and within two hours, they had those two guys, too!"

"No shit. So, you're the hero, huh?"

"You might say that. It was an interesting ordeal."

"I can imagine. My night was interesting."

"I heard. Tell me something. How come every time you need me to help you pull off something, you always wind up doing it without me?"

"I don't know. I guess I'm good…with or without you."

"Bullshit."

"Well, what else could it be? I do wish you could have been a part of it though. Pat was a big help!"

"Yeah? So, my baby was instrumental in your little activities, huh?"

"Man, she was the bomb! Everything went off without a hitch and I'm putting the finishing touches on the rest of this in a few hours. By the way, thanks for letting us use your house."

"What? You're welcome…I guess. I didn't even know we were using my house, but Pat must know about this, right?"

"You know it."

"Well, okay. If she says it's okay, it must be okay. How's Vas?"

"He's good. You'll see him at the house, but when we talk business, I need you to make sure he's out of eyesight and earshot. Might be dangerous and that's why you and Pat need to stay strapped and ready. I got Alphonso and Marco coming over, too…just for security purposes."

"Of course. Say, V, could you do me a favor?"

"Anything, Jr. What is it?"

"I'm tired of this shit. Could you get this over with…today?"

V reached over and fist-bumped his best friend.

"Gladly."

* * *

"Victor. Victor! It's time to leave."

Victor came out of the bathroom and threw a printed T-shirt on. He grabbed his coat and hat and walked past Vance as if he wasn't standing there.

"Wot? You got nonting to say to me?" Vance asked.

"What is there to say? You say it's time to go…let's go, damnit. I'm not finished with my vengeance and I'm going to go ahead and release the rest of my attacks today. Tomorrow, I will be on that flight back to my mansion and I will run that damn firm from there. Chase doesn't work there anymore, so I can't fire him…but I can fire his lady friend, Lisa. And there was something fishy about that Belinda Jett girl. I got a feeling she helps V out a lot. I think I'll fire her just for the hell of it. I'll just bet that damn Dez is probably living it up right about now. Let's go, Vance. I want to get this over with. I need some kind of happiness in my life and when V finds out what I've done, I believe they'll get what they deserve and I'll receive my restitution."

CHAPTER 41

ALL THE FIXINGS

It was like a funeral procession without the emergency flashers on the cars. Everyone seemed to pull up at the same time for this impromptu meeting that V had called. V and Jr. had already made it and had enough time to sit down to a home-cooked meal by Pat and Terri. Moms was there, but they had to force her to sit down and rest. She was so determined to get in that kitchen, but they promised they would let her burn something in a couple of weeks. She didn't like it, but she knew they cared about her. V wanted it to be like a family get-together, so he asked his wife and his 'sister-in-law' if they would cook enough food to feed the usual crew. They agreed and this made V happy. As the cars rolled down the long driveway to the house, one could hear the crunch of the snow and leaves as the tires rolled over them. They all would find a spot to park in front of the house. Vance had never been here before so he was impressed.

"So, Vic. Dis is where you stayed? Brudda, dis is nice!"

"Yeah! I like this! I can see myself living here!" Kerri said.

The brothers had picked Kerri up before coming over to the house, seeing as how V wanted everyone involved to be there.

"Yes, this used to be my house...until it was taken from me."

"How de hell you let someone take your house? As smart as you be, dat's pretty stupid, if you ask me?"

"Nobody asked you, Vance! Both of ya'll, just shut up about this and let's get this shit over with."

The front door opened and it was Patricia.

"Hello, everybody! Hi, Kerri! Hey, Vance! Victor."

"Patricia," Victor said icily.

"Come on in, everybody. Welcome to my humble abode."

"Bullshit." Victor was not happy.

"Aw, Victor, don't be like that. This is a family gathering. The food is ready and we're gonna have a good time!"

"I be ready to eat!" Vance said.

"Me, too," said Kerri.

"Well, come on in. Let me show you to the dining room. Well, kitchen first. I'm not fixing anybody's plate, you know."

"I know that's right. There's nothing but grown folks here, right? Don't worry about me, girl. I know how to fix a plate for myself. I will, however fix Victor a plate, that is if you want me to," Kerri said.

"Yeah, you can. I would say I'm not hungry, but I'd be lying."

"Hell, what's new about that?" V said. He walked up on them while they were still at the door.

"Fu…forget you, V! I'm going to try to be civil, for once."

"Right again, brother. First time for everything, right?" V liked messing with Victor at the moment. He had so much more in store for his older sibling.

"Alright, you two, quit it! Come on."

Everyone followed their host to the kitchen, but V stayed back. Victor looked back over his shoulder at V and gave him an evil grin. V returned the evil grin with a 'knowing what is happening behind the scenes' grin. When the group reached the kitchen, they were greeted with more 'hellos' from the guests who were already in attendance.

"Hello, sons!" Moms greeted.

"Hi, Moms," Vance replied, giving his mother a kiss on the cheek.

"Hello…uh, can I call you Moms, too?" Kerri asked.

"Yes, ma'am, you can. Boy, if you ain't a splitting image of your sister. It's uncanny."

"Yes, it's a good thing we were both brought up right, huh? One of us might have run into trouble."

"Ain't that the truth," Moms replied. "Well, one of you did…in a way."

Moms was referring to Victor and she wasn't trying to cut corners in saying so.

"Victor? You didn't speak," Moms said.

"Didn't I? Oh. I guess I didn't."

"Booyyy! If you weren't my son, I'd…"

"You'd what? Tell a lie so I would have to leave my own home? Tell a lie on me so that I would lose the business I worked so hard to have? Lie in everyone's face that I wasn't who I really was?" Victor blasted back.

"That's enough!" V had finally entered the room where everyone else was. He could see that what Victor was saying was upsetting Moms.

"You forgot about losing your wife, too, dumbass."

"Okay, Moms. You've got your jab in. Now, everyone grab your plates and let's have a nice family dinner. Okay? Victor? Can you do that?" V said. He grabbed Victor by the arm and whispered in his ear, *"Or do I have to kick your ass again?"*

Victor snatched away from V.

"I can do it. Don't touch me no damn more."

"Oh, I'm going to touch you again. You can bet on it and win!"

Everyone except V and Jr., filled their plates with the Southern cooking that was a rarity in the North. Black-eyed peas, macaroni and cheese, candy yams, collard greens and cabbage mix, corn on the cob, fried chicken, sliced ham, beef brisket, fried okra, hot-water cornbread and two big pitchers of sweet tea and lemonade...just in case someone wanted an Arnold Palmer. V called over Alphonso and whispered something in his ear. Alphonso nodded and headed towards his car. He drove away and nobody even noticed he was gone.

Jr. looked at V.

"You ready?" Jr. asked.

"Yep. Get them together."

"Okay, everybody, if you all are finished eating, I'd like to ask you all to come to the den," Jr. announced.

Everyone started grabbing their plates to take to the kitchen. Everyone except Victor, that is.

"Oh, no, leave them. I'll get them later. Please," Pat said.

Once everyone made it to the den, V took over.

"Well, is everyone full?"

They all nodded and some rubbed their stomachs.

"That's good. I'm happy. But after I make...wait, where's Sabino?"

"I'll go look," Jr. said.

"Cool. Well, I guess I'll have to stall. Who wants dessert?"

Only one hand went up. It was Marco.

"Hell, I shoulda known. In due time, Marco. Say, Terri, did you guys make desserts?" V asked.

"Yeah, Sugar. We made apple cobbler, strawberry cake and a German Chocolate cake! We should charge all of ya'll!"

"I know that's right!" Pat chimed in, laughing.

Jr. came in with Sabino.

"Found him sleep in front of the TV."

"Well, welcome, old man!" V said.

"Whatever. Oh. Is it…?"

"Time? Yep, it's time. Now everyone is here so, let me start. The bottom line is this party was thrown with Victor in mind the whole time."

"Me? Why me?" Victor asked.

"Well, we knew you were leaving and we wanted to send you off well. Well. That word just doesn't cut it for me. We wanted to send you off… period."

"You keep saying 'we'. Don't you mean 'you'?"

"As a matter of fact, this is my idea. Have you noticed brother that I have come up with quite a few ideas since I've been out of jail? Hell, how about the one I had when I was in jail? If it weren't for you, I wouldn't have had to come up with none of them, but then again, if it wasn't for you, I wouldn't be as successf…no, not successful. I think a better word would be…uh…wealthy. Wouldn't you say that's a better word, Victor?"

"Kiss my ass!"

"That's what I thought. Now, we all have learned that you and my other brother, Vance, came back to the states to get revenge on just about everyone, right?"

"No! Dat's not right, me brudda! I come to the states for money, not revenge!" Vance said. "I have someting I nevah had before; a brudda I nevah met; a woman I have grown to love and says she loves me; a baby on de way; and a chance to know me real mudda."

"And Father," Sabino added.

"Yeah. I guess someting like dat."

"Okay, Vance. I'll give you some slack. As a matter of fact, you are entitled, if we go by what the Colonel said. He said he owed you, so I will pay you accordingly. First of all, for your cooperation in supplying pertinent information, you can have the $222 million promised to Cassie. If she loves you and you guys plan to be together, she shouldn't mind. I know you'll do the right thing. Also, for helping to kick this whole thing off from the get-go, here is your piggy bank," V said, handing him one.

"Break it in your own privacy and collect your share. Now Victor, is there anything you want to say before I continue?"

"No, please continue, bitch," Victor said to V. V just smiled.

"Bitch, huh? You just won't learn, will you? Okay, Vance, you have a decision to make. You can go back to the islands or you can stay here in the states. I want you to work for me in my security business. I can see how you could be an important asset to my company."

"Really? Where do I stay? Me got no house, you know."

"Yes, you do. You and Cassie have a house. It's right down the road. Isn't it Victor?"

CHAPTER 42

GANG BANG

Victor popped his head up and his eyes got big.
"What the hell are you saying, V? You found my other house? That's my house, damnit!"

"It sure was. And yeah, that's the house I'm talking about. When Terri and I started looking for a place to settle down in, we stumbled across it; found out it was yours, but she didn't want to stay anywhere else you were a part of. Besides, she found a couple of pair of panties that wasn't hers under the bed. Anyway, you sold it to me."

"I did not! When did I sell you my house?"

"Last night, idiot. Do you remember when you thought I was Vance? Did you sign some **more** papers without reading them?"

Victor couldn't take what he was hearing any longer. He jumped up from where he was seated and lunged towards V. Jr., Pat and Marco all pulled their guns and pointed them straight at Victor. Their safeties were on, but no one knew that. Especially not Victor. When he saw the guns, he stopped so suddenly, he almost tripped. He composed himself, brushed off his shirt and went back to his seat. V hadn't even budged from where he stood.

"Now, I have another question for you. Seeing as how you forgot that it was I and not Vance, when I handed you that envelope, did you count it or did you just trust me, as Vance, that is?"

Victor dropped his head.

"Yeah. That's what I thought. How much did I tell you was in that envelope? A starter of a million from the account? Now why, tell me, would Vance give you a million dollars when you owed him? It's one thing I found out about you, Vic. You're not as bright as you come off.

Kinda stupid, if you ask me. And yes sir, this time I am calling you stupid."

"What about all of my shit? My furniture? My studio? My recor...?"

"Your recordings? Everything's just fine. But when you sold the house, you sold the contents, too. Revenge? Shiiit."

"You won't get away with this! I'll sue."

"You signed a contract, son and took money as payment. Legal and binding, fool! By the way, you sold your house for $10,000. Make sure you do count it when you get a chance."

"You bastard! I swear before God, I'll get you for this! I swear!"

"You have to know God before you can even use his name," Moms chimed in.

"That's okay, Moms. Have your fun at my expense. At least I know that you will never be happy again with Thomas Taylor! Yeah, everyone. That man over there is my father, 'Big Daddy' Thomas Taylor. That's a mask and makeup. Sabino is dead and gone and that bastard right there is playing him!"

Those that did not know, looked at Sabino for confirmation.

"It's true. I am not Sabino. I apologize for perpetrating this sham and if I have offended or hurt anyone, I am sorry. I only hope you can forgive me."

"I already have, Dad. The rest of you, that is a personal decision, but know this: he is not a bad person. Love you, man," V said.

"Love you, too, son."

"Yeah, yeah, blah-dy, blayh-dy, blah! As long as I know Moms is hurt and won't be with 'Daddy', as you call him, over there; I'm a happy man," Victor said.

Moms spoke up. "Well, Victor, I see that hurting me was as much a plan as hurting Thomas or even Vincent. Hell, even Terri, am I right?"

"You are so right. You guys did nothing but dessert me and you all deserve to be punished."

"You may even be right, son, but when did you become our judge and executioner? Now about your little hopes about me not being happy, I will say that you are absolutely right. Thomas Taylor and I will never be again. He had his chance and he blew it. Am I hurt? Damn straight! Sorry, everybody. But I have made a decision that even I didn't think I'd make. Thomas Taylor is dead to me."

"Now, that's what I'm talking about! This is fantastic news to me! I needed something to make me feel better and this is what I needed to hear!" Victor said.

"Oh, but let me finish. Thomas Taylor can no longer see me...but Antony Sabino can."

"What?! You're going to see Sabino? That's still Thomas!"

"You see what you see...I'll see what I see. I like Tony and I'm grown."

"You bitch!"

"Now, Victor, I'm going to give you a chance to take that back...right now! That's your mother and no matter what she may have done to you or will do to you, you shouldn't disrespect her that way! Ever!" V said.

"I can't do it, V. Everybody's ganging up on me and I don't have to like it!"

"Naw, man. You're just getting what you thought you were giving. Moms, has he disrespected you like this another time since he came back? I need to know."

"No, I haven't," Victor answered, afraid of the consequences.

"Well...come to think of it, he did. At the Gala."

"What did I do to you...or say?" Victor asked.

"You told me to 'kiss your ass'. Remember that?"

Victor started smiling, but quickly stopped. The front gate buzzed the intercom and Pat went to see who it was. When she came back, she was smiling.

"Who was that?" Jr. asked.

"You'll see," she said, still smiling.

"Well, Victor, you have made my next decision even easier, although I thought I would give you a break. But just to show some compassion and not embarrass you in front of everyone...not that you're not already embarrassed...I'm going to allow you to find this last one out when you get home in a few hours."

"A few hours?! My flight doesn't leave until the morning!"

"Shiiit, your flight has been changed. You leave in...what...2 hours? You already know the drill. Marco and Alphonso will accompany you to your hotel room to get your shit and to the airport so you can git. Right, Marco?"

"You got it, boss," Marco replied.

Alphonso entered back into the house and the room but he wasn't alone. Cassie was there, as well. When Vance saw her, he leapt to his feet and ran to her. They embraced and he kissed her on the forehead. Alphonso winked at V and was reciprocated with the same. Victor was beside himself and at a loss of words at the moment.

"What about me? I'm pregnant with Victor's baby! If he leaves, do I have to leave, too?" Kerri asked.

"Naw, girl. You can stay here with Jr. and I…and our baby," Pat said.

Jr. looked up abruptly at Pat.

"Did you say, 'our baby'? Pat, are you pregnant?"

"I'm sorry, Jr. It just came out. I wanted to tell you alone, but…I guess I got caught up."

"No, baby, you don't have to apologize. I'm ecstatic! Did you hear that, V? I'm gonna be a daddy!"

"I heard, man. Congratulations!"

"Aw, shit, another damn baby," Victor said. "You're not really going to have that baby, are you Kerri? I mean, you won't have no man or father around for the child."

Kerri's eyes began to swell up with tears. She thought Victor cared for her. She was finding out the hard way, that Victor cared for no one but himself.

"Don't you worry about Kerri or her baby, Victor! She has a family now; a village. She is not by herself in this and that should be the last of your worries!" Terri spoke up, boldly.

"Terri, why don't you just shut the hell…?"

"Naw, Victor, I'm not afraid of you anymore! You're just a bully and all you try to do is hurt people so that you can feel better about yourself. Now I believe I can speak for everyone in this room when I say, 'Kiss our asses, Victor Taylor!' And you can get your ass gone from here as soon as possible. Bye, Felicia!"

V was grinning and quite proud of his wife for standing up to her former husband. He nodded to the Punishers, but instead of grabbing Victor and taking him out, they beckoned for him to go with them. He stood up looking defeated, but still knew he had one more card to play. As he got ready to leave the room, V spoke to him one more time.

"Victor? I hope you will eventually learn that most times when you try to get revenge on someone, it won't pay off and you will wind up being the one that revenge is played on. I hope that if you ever come back again, you will be a changed man. You're smart, you have style and hell, you look like me, so you're good-looking, too."

"Yah, mon, me, too!" Vance said.

"Think about it, man. You're too good to have allowed the things that happened to you occur. All because you wanted to cause pain. You're the biggest asshole I know, but I still love you, man."

"Yeah? One thing I've noticed about all of you; you say you love me, but you have the strangest ways of showing it. You lie on me and you take my shit. It's all bullshit, if you ask me," Victor replied.

With that, Victor headed out. Before he could make it to the door, Vasyl came running up behind him.

"Uncle Victory? You leaving? Where you going?"

Terri started to go get Vas, but V stopped her.

"Hold up, baby. He's okay," V said.

"Hey, little fellow. What's your name?" Victor asked.

"Vasyl. It means brave. What does your name mean?"

"It means conqueror. Yeah."

"Cool! So, you leaving? When you coming back?"

"I don't know, kid. How do you know my name anyway?"

"My Daddy always shows me a picture of you and I can tell you apart by your eyes."

"Yeah?"

"Yep. My Daddy is always bragging about you. I think you're his hero."

"Is that so?" Victor said, looking past Vas at his brother V. "Well, look kid, I gotta go. I'll see you again and when I do, you can tell me what you've been up to. Okay?"

"Okay, Uncle Victory. See you later. You be good, okay?"

This was the first time Victor was touched by another human being. He wiped his eyes and headed out the door with Marco and Alphonso.

Uncle Victory. Wow, he thought.

"Well, Vance have you made your decision?" V asked.

"I 'ave. When do me start?"

"First things first. You haven't even eaten any dessert yet. Taste them and let my girls know which one you like best!" Moms said.

"Dat, I can do!"

CHAPTER 43

SURPRISE!

"Wow. What an ordeal, huh?" Terri asked V while they were on their way to their home.

"For sure. But Victor got what he deserved. He still doesn't know the last thing I did."

"What's that?"

"Let's give it a couple of days before I tell you, okay? Trust me, it's gonna hurt."

"I guess I can wait. But what happened to trust and honesty with us?"

"See, now you're trying to use that against me. That's not fair. But, please, can't you wait?"

"Yeah, Babes. I can wait. I sure did want my sister to stay with me instead of somewhere else."

"That wouldn't have worked at all."

"Why not?"

"Because then, I wouldn't have been able to tell you two apart. Here I come, grabbing who I think is my wife, and it's my sister-in-law. Too complicated for me. That is until she started showing. Hell, that would be the only way I would be able to make a distinction. You should know all about it."

"Yeah, you're right. I would have been too pissed if I walked in and saw you two smooching. She might mistake you for Victor and you would mistake her for me. No…I'm not having that! Well, at least I'll be able to see her, huh? Are we going to be able to help her with the baby?"

"I already got that covered. Another surprise…for you and her."

"Well, if you think about it, it probably was best that Victor wouldn't be around anyway."

"Right. And Pat and Jr. How about that, eh?"

"What's that? Them having a baby? I know, right? The only thing that might be worse than Kerri, Pat **and** Cassie being pregnant, would be if **I** were pregnant. I say worse, but you know what I mean, right? I don't really mean 'worse'. I mean, it's not a bad thing when someone has a baby, is it? Hell, for them or whoever, a baby could make a positive difference in their lives, don't you agree? Some might even say a blessing. I know Vas is a blessing for us. I love him and I love his father. Having a baby is not the end of the world, is it? On the contrary, it's the beginning of life. Can you imagine the ones who have abortions just because they didn't want a baby? Or even adoption. Or even selling a child. I mean, to me, all that's crazy. Do you know what I'm talking about, V? I'm just saying, if I were pregnant along with all those other ladies having a baby…man, that really would be some shit, huh, V?"

V got silent for a moment. He pulled up to their house, stopped the car at the front door, killed the engine and looked at his wife.

"Terri?"

"Uh huh."

"That was a lot of talking you just did. Can I ask you a question?"

"Uh huh."

"Baby…are you…preg…?"

"Pregnant? Me?" Terri asked.

"Yeah…you."

Terri turned her head towards the window.

"Uh huh."

* * *

Victor rolled up in his taxicab pickup, to his Jamaican home, straight from the airport. He sported a smile on his face that he just couldn't seem to get rid of. He smiled so much, his face began to hurt. Even though a lot was taken from him, he couldn't get over the fact that in the end, he would still get his firm back and receive the proceeds from the work being done. He walked up to his front door and before he could open it, Dez flung it open.

"Hey, mon! Welcome home, Mistah Taylor!"

More Wrongs: The Revenge

"What's up, Dez? Damn, Dez you weren't sleep? It's three in the morning. I guess you've been living it up since I've been gone, huh?"

"Oh, no sir. No, no, no. Dez has been good," he lied.

"Yeah, I'll bet. Grab these bags and take them to my bedroom, hear?"

"Yeah, mon, right on it."

While Dez went to grab the bags, Victor went in his house and headed for his den. There was a basket placed in there that Dez collected all of his mail in. Victor started going through it. He was hoping to find something related to the sale of the firm back to him. He started to get excited. It was the wee hours of the 23rd, and Victor had always had his payments from his firm to be distributed to his employees and to the owner on the 22nd of every month. If things went as planned, he would at least get a statement as to how much would be deposited to his bank account. He would look at his bank account shortly, but now he wanted to see what he made on paper. He made sure that everything would be express-mailed to him that had to do with his transaction. While going through the mail, he found an express letter that came from V's business address. COC Securities, 62863 Baker Street, NY, NY 10550. He opened it first.

Dear Victor,

I sent this letter Thursday, the 20th of December, knowing it would probably beat you home. I just wanted you to know that you are a cold-blooded bastard. I would like to allow you to see what you did, because you don't seem to see it when you do it.
1. You were going to let me die in prison for a crime you knew I didn't commit.
2. You tried to steal my money. (Could have just asked, dumbass)
3. You tried to hurt Moms. (heart attack. That's pretty bad, brother)
4. You tried to make sure Moms and Daddy never got together again. (You sorta succeeded there.)
5. You tried to break up my relationship with Terri.
6. You tried to sleep with my wife! (Yeah, she told me.)
7. You tried to buy back your firm. (That's right, TRIED!)
8. You even used Cassie. (I still care about her. My love is for Terri, but Cassie is still a friend.)

9. You were even going to blow up Pat & Jr's house! (Yeah, we swept the office…found your BAT. If my son, Vas would have been there and it happened, you wouldn't be reading this letter.)
10. You forgot about family first.

Now, it's time to teach you a lesson. As you can see, when you focus on hurting others, look how things end up. I must say this: I have never in my life seen you as sloppy and unprepared as you have been when trying to get back at someone. You've got to learn to forgive. Jimi Hendrix said "When the power of love overcomes the love of power, then we will all know peace." So, let me tell you how this ends for you: Your mansion; you lost it to me and I gave it to Jr. and Pat. Your other house; you sold it to me and I gave it to Vance and Cassie. You purchased two cars. Vance and Kerri both needed transportation, so thanks a lot! Vance got his pay from your account that you two agreed upon. (Can't believe you didn't think to change accounts before he got his hands on it. Sloppy!) That's $100 million…gone. Then, you paid $265 million for the purchase of a law firm that didn't buy a law firm. When you finish this letter, look at your contract and your bank account. That, my brother, was a donation. Thanks again. I'll take that $265 million and use it to support your new baby and use what's left to start a scholarship for all of our kids. Of course, it will be in your name. The Victor Taylor Scholarship Fund! You should be proud! Maybe not. The Elaine Taylor Scholarship Fund sounds better. Now, if I am not mistaken, when you started, you had right at $368 million dollars, right? You should have a little under $2 million now. But if you think that's bad, guess what? It gets worse. I've pulled some strings and had you disbarred. All that work and school for nothing. Shame, shame, shame. I'm not through. Sometime today, you should be getting a visit from the IRS. A couple of friends of mine. Something about unreported funds. Who knows how much they will take? So, now I'm thinking to myself, I'm preaching to my brother about forgiveness and family first and being kind and here I am trying to hurt my own brother. What kind of example am I being? And then I think to myself, you're damned right I'm trying to hurt you! You deserve it. You wanted to see what revenge looked like, so here you go! I would love to see you be successful, because you're a Taylor but you're going to have to start over as…what? The most successful sanitation worker of all time?

Ha ha! Anyway, if you **ever** think about getting revenge on me and my family again; brother, think again. Next time, I'll leave your ass homeless!

Sincerely,
Vincent Taylor
Vincent Taylor

P. S. And If you think I'm playing, you can look at your contract and your bank account now. Bitch.

Victor crumbled the letter in his hands and ran to where his luggage was. He pulled out the folder that held the contract for the law firm. He had already read over the contract twice and it seemed to have everything needed to make the sale legal and binding. When he unfolded the contract, he could have cried. There was nothing on the contract but his signature. He insisted on using his own pen. Everyone else used the pen that had the same type of ink the contract had on it: disappearing. He looked at each page, only to find disappointment and white paper with no black writing anywhere. He knew it was disappearing ink, because he had used it years ago in a deal taking everything a man owned and leading to that man's suicide. He had wired $265 million in return for nothing but blank pieces of paper that obtained his signature only. He went to his computer and pulled up his bank statement. There it was; plain as day; his balance. $1.4 million dollars. Victor was devastated. He couldn't even curse his brother at the moment; his throat was too dry to talk.
Damn, V. You're good, he thought.

He went back to the den and looked through the rest of his mail. There was nothing there from or about the firm. There was, however a letter from the American Bar Association. He didn't even bother to open it. He knew V told the truth about disbarment. At the very bottom, though there was a letter with no return address on it. It was trimmed in gold, and it looked important, so he opened it, hoping it contained some good news…anything. It read:

Hey, Vic!
I got all your recordings you put together in your personal studio! This is some good stuff! You have hits after hits and I would love to fund

you if you are ready to go into the music industry. Let me know. You don't have to call me or write me, just say it out loud. I'll hear you.

Sincerely,
A Music Lover!

Victor stared at the letter for what seemed to be minutes. He then looked up towards his ceiling and yelled, "Okay. I'm ready."

"Wot mon?" Dez called out in response.

"Nothing, Dez. I got it," he yelled back.

There was only silence. Dez was busy upstairs, putting away Victor's belongings.

"Now what do I do?" Victor asked himself. He decided to watch TV. He knew there was nothing he could do but face the IRS people head on when they finally arrived. He certainly wouldn't run. He was way too tired for that. He had done prison, even though it would not show up on his record, so he was certain he could handle that if he had to. As he watched TV, he started to nod off to sleep, but was startled when his cell phone rang. He pulled it out of his pants pocket, looked at it, but didn't recognize the number. He started not to answer, but thought, *what the hell.*

"Hello?"

"Are you really ready?" a voice asked.

"Ready for what?" Victor answered.

"Ready to start your music career! What else?"

"Yeah. I'm ready. Who is this?"

"This is the Colonel. Let's start this business transaction off right, okay? How much money do you need me to front you?"

"The Colonel? Casey? I thought you were…aw, shit! Was I played?"

"You were. Don't feel bad. Others were, also. I would have never called you, but these tracks you laid down are the bomb!"

"Well, I'll be a fucking monkey's uncle! So…you're seriously interested, or am I being played again?"

"I'm serious, dude. You have some nice…no, better than nice, shit! How much?"

"Huh?"

"How much do you need me to front you? I understand you've got some visitors coming soon, correct?"

"Yeah. Damn, man, you do know everything, don't you?!"

"Yep."

"Okay. Make me this deal. When they come and leave, they will let me know what I owe. If I can call you…hell, or just call out…you'll cover my bill?"

"Sure."

"No matter how much?"

"Not a problem for me. I got it. We have to get that shit out of the way first and then we can talk business. You don't realize what you have, do you?"

"What's that?"

"The tools to blow up the music industry. Trust me. With your talents and my money, you could be the most successful artist of all time!"

"So, what you're telling me is I'm good, huh?"

"Oh, yes! You're very good! Better than you probably think you are."

This made Victor beam on the inside. It had been a while since someone complemented him…on anything.

"And also, you're telling me, that you and I would be business partners, right?"

"Right again. But I'm not stupid, Victor. You could take my front money and be done with me. But then again, I hope you're not stupid, either. You should know by now, you can't run and you can't hide from me and besides, you could possibly be throwing away your chance to multi-millions! So, what do you say? Do you want to go into partnership with me or not? I don't have all day so, let me know. And by the way, the front money is part of the agreement."

"How long do I have to give you my answer?"

"Uh…now. Right now, or forget it. I have your music, but you can't prove it's yours. I'll just put someone else's name on it and reap the benefits."

"That doesn't leave me with much of a choice, does it? Hell, if I have to give you an answer now…it's yes! Let's do it!"

"Cool! I'll wait to hear from you later today. Oh, and also, if you take a match and hold it up to the back of that letter I sent you, my personal phone number will show up. Call me if you're serious. I know I am. And make sure you tell those IRS guys, you got it. Got it?"

"Yeah. Got it."

With that the Colonel hung up. Victor thought about his recent downfall and his turnaround fortunate circumstance. *This time, if I get on top, I'm going to stay on top!* he thought. He nodded. He smiled. He dreamed…again.

ABOUT THE AUTHOR

Anthony Baker has done television, movies and has even acted on the live stage. Born and raised in Little Rock, AR, he now resides in Benton, AR along with his wife, Vanessa. His desire is to entertain the reader with stories that paint a picture, with a few twists involved. He challenges his audience to #staywoke.